"I want to tal
because I've
find him."

"You're not meeting Connor until you tell me what I need to know! What was I to you? A one-night stand? *A hooker?*" she slung furiously. "Or a girlfriend?"

With pronounced cool, Gianni came upright to face her. "No to all of the above. Leave this for another day, *cara,*" he advised quietly, incisive dark-as-night eyes resting on the revealing clenching and unclenching of her hands. "When the time's right, I'll tell you everything you want to know."

"I'll ask you one more time before I walk out of here…what was I to you?"

Gianni expelled his breath in a slow hiss. "You were my mistress."

Amnesia

**What the memory has lost,
the body never forgets**

An electric chemistry with
a disturbingly familiar stranger...
A reawakening of passions long forgotten...
And a compulsive desire to get to know this
stranger all over again!

A compelling miniseries from Harlequin
Presents®, featuring our top-selling authors.
Look out for more AMNESIA stories in 2001!

Lynne Graham

THE SICILIAN'S MISTRESS

Amnesia

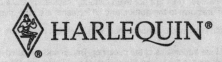

HARLEQUIN®

TORONTO • NEW YORK • LONDON
AMSTERDAM • PARIS • SYDNEY • HAMBURG
STOCKHOLM • ATHENS • TOKYO • MILAN • MADRID
PRAGUE • WARSAW • BUDAPEST • AUCKLAND

ISBN 0-373-12139-3

THE SICILIAN'S MISTRESS

First North American Publication 2000.

Visit us at www.eHarlequin.com

Printed in U.S.A.

CHAPTER ONE

STUDIOUSLY ignoring Faith's troubled expression, Edward smiled. 'I never dreamt that Mother would make us such a generous offer—'

Faith sucked in a deep, steadying breath. 'I know, *but*—'

'It makes perfect sense. Why go to the expense of buying another property when there's ample space for us all at Firfield?'

At that precise moment Edward's flight was called. Immediately he rose to his feet and lifted his briefcase. 'We'll talk it over when I get back.'

Faith stood up. A slim, beautiful blonde of diminutive height, she had sapphire-blue eyes, flawless skin and wore her hair in a restrained French plait. 'I'll see you to the gate.'

Her fiancé shook his well-groomed fair head. 'Not much point. I don't know why you bothered coming to see me off anyway,' he remarked rather drily. 'I'm only going to be away for three days.'

Edward strode off and was soon lost from view in the crowds. Faith left the café at a slower pace, genuinely appalled at the announcement Edward had just made. They were getting married in four months and they had been house-hunting for the past three. Now Faith sensed that as far as Edward was concerned the hunt was over: his mother had offered to share her spacious home with them.

It was a really ghastly idea, Faith acknowledged in guilty dismay. Edward's mother didn't like her, but she carefully concealed her hostility. Mrs Benson was no more fond of Faith's two-year-old son, Connor. But then the fact that Faith was an unmarried mother had first fuelled the older

5

woman's dislike, Faith conceded ruefully as she walked back through the airport.

Her troubled eyes skimmed through the hurrying crowds. Suddenly she stiffened, her gaze narrowing, her head twisting back of its own volition to retrace that visual sweep. She found herself focusing on a strikingly noticeable man standing on the far side of the concourse in conversation with another. As her heartbeat thumped deafeningly in her ears, she faltered into complete stillness.

The compulsion to stare was as overwhelming as it was inexplicable. The man was very tall and very dark. His hard, bronzed features were grave, but not so grave that one glance was not sufficient to make her aware that he was stunningly handsome. Her tummy somersaulted. A fevered pound of tension began to build up pressure behind her temples.

A smooth dark overcoat hung negligently from his wide shoulders. He looked rich, super-sophisticated, that cool aura of razor-edged elegance cloaking immense power. Perspiration dampened her skin. Sudden fear and confusion tore at her as she questioned what she was doing. A wave of dizziness ran over her.

Simultaneously, the stranger turned his arrogant dark head and looked directly at her, only to freeze. The fierce intensity with which those brilliant dark eyes zeroed in on her stilled figure disconcerted her even more. But at that point the nausea churning in her stomach forced a muffled moan from her parted lips. Dragging her attention from him, Faith rushed off in search of the nearest cloakroom.

She wasn't actually sick, as she had feared. But as she crept back out of the cubicle she had locked herself in and approached the line of sinks she was still trembling. Most of all, she was bewildered and shaken by her own peculiar behaviour. What on earth had possessed her to behave like that? What on earth had prompted her to stop dead and gape like some infatuated schoolgirl at a complete stranger?

Infatuated? She questioned the selection of that particular

word and frowned with unease, the way she always did when a thought that didn't seem quite *her* came into her mind. But she wasn't feeling well. Maybe she was feverish, coming down with one of those viruses that could strike with such rapidity.

There had to be some good reason why a total stranger should inspire her with fear…unless he reminded her of somebody she had once known. She tensed. That was highly unlikely, she decided just as quickly, and began to scold herself for her overreaction to a fleeting incident.

But she knew what was the matter with her. She understood all too well the source of her basic insecurity. But *that* was something she had learnt to put behind her and never ever dwell on these days. With conscious care, Faith suppressed the scary stirrings at the back of her mind and blanked them out again.

But what if she *had* once known that man? The worrying apprehension leapt out of Faith's subconscious before she could block it again. Aghast, she stared blindly into space, suddenly plunged into a world of her own, a blank, nebulous world of terrifying uncertainty which she had believed left far behind her. *The lost years…what about them?*

A crowd of noisy teenagers jostled her at the sinks, springing her back into awareness again. She blinked rapidly, once, twice, snatched in a shuddering breath to steady herself. Discomfited by her uncomfortably emotional frame of mind, she averted her head and shook it slightly. You saw some really interesting people at airports, she told herself squarely. Her attention had been momentarily distracted and she wasn't feeling too good. That was all it had been.

But when Faith vacated the cloakroom and turned back into the main concourse, she found her path unexpectedly blocked.

'Milly…?' A dark, accented voice breathed with noticeable stress.

Faith glanced up, and it was a very long way up, and met flashing dark eyes so cold and deep her heart leapt straight into her throat. It was the same guy she had been staring at ten minutes earlier! Her feet froze to the floor in shock.

'*Madre di Dio…*' The stranger stared fixedly down at her, his deep, accented drawl like an icy hand dancing down her taut spine. 'It *is* you!'

Faith gazed up at him in frank surprise and sudden powerful embarrassment. She took a backward step. 'Sorry, I think you've got the wrong person.'

'Maybe you wish I had.' The intimidating stranger gazed down at her from his incredibly imposing height, slumbrous dark eyes roving so intently over her face that colour flooded her drawn cheeks. '*Dio*…you still blush. How do you do that?' he drawled very, very softly.

'Look, I don't know you, and I'm in a hurry,' Faith responded in an evasive, mortified mutter, because she couldn't help wondering if her own foolish behaviour earlier had encouraged him to believe that she was willing to be picked up.

Eyes the colour of rich, dark golden honey steadily widened and her heartbeat started to thump at what felt like the base of her throat, making it difficult for her to breathe. 'You don't know me?' he repeated very drily. 'Milly, this is Gianni D'Angelo you're dealing with, and running scared with a really stupid story won't dig you out of the big deep hole you're in!'

'You don't know me. You've made a mistake,' Faith told him sharply.

'No mistake, Milly. I could pick you out of a thousand women in the dark,' Gianni D'Angelo murmured even more drily, his wide, sensual mouth curling with growing derision. 'So, if the nose job was supposed to make you unrecognisable, it's failed. And what sad soap opera did you pick this crazy pretence out of? You're in enough trouble without this childish nonsense!'

Her dark blue eyes huge in receipt of such an incomprehensible address, Faith spluttered, 'A nose job? For goodness' sake—'

'You have a lot of explaining to do, and I intend to conduct this long-overdue conversation somewhere considerably more private than the middle of an airport,' he asserted grittily. 'So let's get out of here before some paparazzo recognises me!'

As Faith attempted to sidestep him he spontaneously matched her move and blocked her path again. She studied him in disbelief. 'P-please get out of my way...' she stammered, fear and confusion now rising like a surging dark tide inside her.

'No.'

'You're mad...if you don't get out of my way, I'll scream!'

He reeled back a full step, a deep frown-line of impressive incredulity hardening his lean, strong features. 'What the hell is going on here?' he demanded with savage abruptness.

Faith broke through the gap he had left by the wall and surged past him at frantic speed.

A hand as strong and sure as an iron vice captured her wrist before she got more than two feet away. '*Accidenti*...where do you think you're going?' he questioned in angry disbelief, curving his infinitely larger hand right round her clenched fingers.

'I'll report you to the police for harassing me!' Faith gasped. 'Let go of me!'

'Don't be ridiculous...' He gazed unfathomably down into her frightened and yet strangely blank eyes and suddenly demanded with raw, driven urgency, '*What's the matter with you?*'

Faith spun a frantic glance around herself. Only her instinctive horror at the idea of creating a seriously embarrassing public scene restrained her from a noisy outburst. '*Please* let go of me!' she urged fiercely.

The ring on her engagement finger scored his palm as she tried to pull free. Without warning he flipped her hand around in the firm hold of his and studied the small diamond solitaire she wore. A muscle jerked tight at the corner of his bloodlessly compressed lips, shimmering flaring eyes flying up again to her taut face.

'*Now* I understand why you're acting like a madwoman!' he grated, with barely suppressed savagery.

And Faith's self-discipline just snapped, right then and there. She flung back her head and tried to call out for assistance, but her vocal cords were knotted so tight with stress only a suffocated little squawk emerged. But surprisingly that was sufficient. Gianni D'Angelo, as he had called himself, dropped her hand as if she had burnt him and surveyed her in almost comical astonishment.

Shaking like a leaf, Faith backed away. 'I'm not this Milly you're looking for...never seen you before in my life, never want to see you again...'

And she rushed away her tummy tied up in sick knots again, her head pounding, a kind of nameless terror controlling her. She raced across the endless car park as if she had wings, and then fell, exhausted, to a slower pace, breathless and winded, heartbeat thundering. Crazy, crazy man, frightening her like that all because she resembled some poor woman who had clearly got out while the going was good. Gianni D'Angelo. She didn't recognise that name. And why should she?

But wasn't it strange that he should have attracted *her* attention first? And only then had he approached her. Almost as if he genuinely had recognised her...

As her apprehensions rose to suffocating proportions release from fear came in the guise of an obvious fact. Of course he *couldn't* have recognised her! She couldn't believe that she had ever been the kind of person to run around using a false name! And she was Faith Jennings, the only child of Robin and Davina Jennings. True, she might have been a difficult teenager, but then that wasn't that uncommon, and her parents had long since forgiven her for the awful anxiety she had once caused them.

Half an hour later, sitting in her little hatchback car in heavy morning rush-hour traffic, Faith took herself to task for the overwrought state she was in. Here she was, supposedly a mature adult of twenty-six, reacting like a frightened teenager desperate to rush home to her parents for support. And yet what had happened? Virtually nothing. A case of mistaken identity with a stubborn foreigner unwilling to accept his error! That was all it had been. A nose job, for heaven's sake!

And yet as she gazed through the windscreen she no longer saw the traffic lights; she saw Gianni D'Angelo, his lean, bronzed features imposed on a mind that for some reason could focus on nothing else. As furiously honking car horns erupted behind her Faith flinched back to the present and belatedly drove on, strain and bemusement stamping her troubled face.

Gianni D'Angelo stared fixedly out of the giant corner window of his London office. An impressive view of the City's lights stretched before him but he couldn't see it.

His sane mind was telling him that even twelve hours on he was still in the grip of shock, and that self-control was everything, but he wanted to violently punch walls with the frustrated anger of disbelief. He had searched for Milly for so long. He had almost given up hope. He certainly hadn't expected her to do something as dumb and childish as try and pretend she didn't know him, and then compound her past offences by attempting to run away again. And why hadn't it occurred to her that he would have her followed before she got ten feet away from him?

Milly, whom he'd always called Angel. And instantly Gianni was beset by a thousand memories that twisted his guts even after three years of rigorous rooting out of such images. He saw Milly jumping out of a birthday cake dressed as an angel, tripping over her celestial robes and dropping her harp. Milly, impossibly beautiful but horrendously clumsy when she was nervous. Milly, who had given him his first and only taste of what he had dimly imagined must be a home life...

And you loved it, you stupid bastard! Gianni's lean hands suddenly clenched into powerful fists. Punishing himself for recalling only pleasant things, Gianni made himself relive the moment he had found his precious pregnant Angel in bed with his kid brother, Stefano. That had put a whole new slant on the joys of home and family life. Until that moment of savage truth he hadn't appreciated just how much he had trusted her. And instead of proposing marriage, as he had planned, he had ended up taking off with another woman. What else could he have done in the circumstances?

He had wanted to kill them both. For the first time he had understood the concept of a crime of passion. The only two people he had ever allowed close had deceived and betrayed him. A boy of nineteen and a girl/woman only a couple of years older. The generation gap had been there, even though he had been too blind to acknowledge it, he reflected with smouldering bitterness. And naturally Stefano had adored her. Everybody had adored Milly.

Milly, who had called him on the slightest pretext every day and never once failed to tell him how much she loved him. So she had spent a lot of time alone. But business had always come first, and he had never promised more than he had delivered. He had been straight. He had even been faithful. And how many single men in his position were wholly faithful to a mistress?

As a knock sounded on the door Gianni wheeled round and fixed his attention with charged expectancy on his London security chief, Dawson Carter. His child, he thought with ferocious satisfaction. Milly *had* to have had his child. And, whatever happened, he would use that child as leverage. Whether she liked it or not, Milly was coming back to him...

'Well?' he prodded with unconcealed impatience.

Dawson surveyed his incredibly rich and ruthless employer and started to sweat blood. Gianni D'Angelo ran one of the most powerful electronic empires in the world. He was thirty-two. He had come up from nothing. He was tough, streetwise, and brilliant in business. He didn't like or expect disappointments. He had even less tolerance for mysteries.

'If this woman *is* Milly Henner—' Dawson began with wary quietness.

Gianni stilled. 'What do you mean *if*?' he countered with raw incredulity.

Dawson grimaced. 'Gianni…if it is her, she's living under another name, and she's been doing it successfully for a very long time.'

'That's insane, and utterly impossible!' Gianni asserted in instant dismissal.

'Three years ago, Faith Jennings was found by the side of a country road in Cornwall. She had been seriously injured and she had no identification. She was the victim of a hit and run. The police think she was robbed after the accident—'

'*Dio!*' Gianni exclaimed in shaken interruption.

'But she *was* pregnant at the time of the accident,' Dawson confirmed. 'And she does have a child.'

Gianni drew in a stark breath, incisive dark eyes flaming to bright gold in anticipation. 'So the child must be two and a half…right? A girl or a boy?' he prompted with fierce impatience.

'A little boy. She calls him Connor. He'll be three in May. He was born before his mother came out of the coma she was in.'

Gianni screened his unusually revealing eyes as he mulled over those bald facts. 'So…' he murmured then, without any expression at all. 'Explain to me how Milly Henner could possibly be living under another woman's name.'

'It was a long time before she was able to speak for herself, but she was apparently wearing a rather unusual bracelet. Her face had been pretty badly knocked about and she needed surgery.' For the first time in his life Dawson saw his employer wince, and was sincerely shaken by the evidence of this previously unsuspected vein of sensitivity. 'So as a first move the police gave a picture of the bracelet to the press. She was swiftly identified as a teenager who had run away from home when she was sixteen. Her parents came forward and identified her—'

'But Milly doesn't *have* parents alive!' Gianni cut in abrasively.

'This woman never recovered her memory after the hit and run, Gianni. She's a total amnesiac—'

'A total amnesiac?' Gianni broke in, with raised brows of dubious enquiry.

'It's rare, but it does happen,' Dawson assured him ruefully. 'I spoke to a nurse at the hospital where she was treated. They still remember her. When she finally recovered consciousness her mind was a blank, and when her parents took her home she still knew nothing but what they had told her about her past. I gather they also discouraged her from seeking further treatment. The medics were infuriated by their interference but powerless to act.'

'Normal people do not take complete strangers home and keep them as their daughters for three years,' Gianni informed him with excessive dryness.

'I should add that the parents hadn't seen or heard from their missing daughter in seven years, but were still unshakeable in their conviction that the young woman with the bracelet was their child—'

'Seven years?' Gianni broke in.

'The police did try to run a check on dental records, but the surgery which the daughter attended before she disappeared had burnt down, and the most her retired dentist could recall was that she had had excellent teeth, just like the lady in the hospital bed. This is a very well-known story in the town where Faith Jennings lives—her miraculous return home in spite of all the odds.'

'There was no return, miraculous or otherwise…that *was* Milly at the airport! Seven years…' Gianni mused with incredulous bite. 'And Milly was in a coma, at the mercy of people no better than kidnappers!'

Dawson cleared his throat. 'The parents are respectable, comfortably off—the father owns a small engineering plant. If there's been a mistake, it can only have been a genuine one, and most probably due to wishful thinking.'

Gianni was unimpressed. 'While Milly was still ill, that's possible, but when she began to recover they must've have started to suspect the truth, so why didn't they *do* anything?' he demanded in a seething undertone. 'What about the fiancé?'

'Edward Benson. A thirty-eight-year-old company accountant.'

Gianni lounged back against the edge of his desk like a panther about to spring. 'An accountant,' he derided between clenched teeth.

'He's her father's second-in-command,' Dawson filled in. 'Local gossip suggests that the engagement is part of a business package.'

'Check me into a hotel down there.' Gianni straightened, all emotion wiped from his lean, strong face, eyes ice-cool shards of threat. 'I think it's time I got to meet my son. And isn't that going to put the cat among the pigeons?'

Dawson tried not to picture the onslaught of Gianni, his powerful personality, his fleet of limos and his working entourage without whom he went nowhere on a small, peaceful English town...and the woman who against all reason and self-preservation had contrived to forget her intimate involvement with one of the world's richest and most influential tycoons. A lot of people had a lot of shock coming their way...

'So you just tell Edward you *refuse* to live with his mother!' Louise Barclay met Faith's aghast look and simply laughed. A redhead with green eyes and loads of freckles, Louise looked as if she was in her twenties but she was actually well into her thirties, and the divorced mother of two rumbustious teenage boys.

'Sometimes you're such a wimp, Faith,' Louise teased.

'I'm not—'

'You are when it comes to your own needs. All your energy goes into keeping other people happy, living the life *they* think you should live! Your parents act like they own you body and soul, and Edward's not much better!' Louise informed her in exasperation.

Faith stiffened. Louise was her best friend and her business partner, but she had little understanding of the burden of guilt that Faith carried where her parents were concerned. 'It's not like that—'

'Oh, yes, it is.' Louise watched Faith carefully package a beautiful bouquet for delivery and leant back against the shop counter. 'I'm always watching you struggle to be all things to all people. Once you wanted to be a gardener. Your parents didn't fancy that, so here you are in a prissy flower shop.'

Faith laughed. 'Alongside you.'

'But this *was* my dream. And if you don't watch out, you're going to end up living with old Ma Benson. She will cunningly contrive, without Edward ever noticing, to make your home life the equivalent of a daily dance on a bed of sharpened nails!' the lively redhead forecast with conviction. 'You think I haven't noticed how stressed-out and quiet you've been since Edward dropped this on you the day before yesterday?'

Faith turned her head away. For once, Louise was barking up the wrong tree. Faith hadn't told anybody about that incident at the airport, but she still couldn't get it out of her mind. Her mother didn't like to be reminded that her daughter was an amnesiac, and got upset whenever Faith referred to that particular part of the past. Her attitude was understandable: after running away, Faith hadn't once got in touch to ease her parents' distress.

How could she ever have been so selfish and uncaring that she had failed to make even a single phone call to reassure them that she was at least still alive? Conscience had given Faith a strong need to do whatever she could to please her parents in an effort to make up for her past mistakes.

She was also painfully aware that both her parents viewed those missing years as a Pandora's box best left sealed. As far as they were concerned, seven years on she had turned up again, pregnant, unmarried and seemingly destitute. Nobody she might have known during that period had listed her as missing. Those bald realities suggested that prior to the accident she had been homeless, unemployed, not in a stable relationship and bereft of any true friends. Frankly, she'd been desperately lucky to have forgiving parents willing to take her home and help her back to normality again, she acknowledged humbly.

Only what was normality? Faith wondered, with the lonely regret of someone who had learnt not to discuss her secret fears and insecurities with anyone. It could never be *normal* to possess not one single memory of what she'd been told she'd lost—the first twenty-three years of her life. But if she wanted people to feel comfortable with her, if she wanted people to forget that strange past and treat her like everybody else, she always had to pretend that that vast gaping hole inside her memory banks was no longer any big deal…

'A fresh start.' In the early days of her convalescence that had been a much-used parental phrase, the implication being that an inability to recall those years might well prove an unexpected blessing. So Faith had concentrated instead on trying to retrieve childhood memories. She had dutifully studied the photo albums of the much-loved and indulged daughter who had grown into a plump teenager with a sullen face, defiant blue eyes and make-up like war paint. Self-conscious about her weight, the teenage Faith hadn't liked photos, so there had only been a handful after the age of twelve.

Faith had walked through the schools she had once attended, met the teachers, wandered round the town where she had grown up and paid several awkward visits to former schoolfriends, always willing her blank brain to remember, recognise, sense even token familiarity...

Repetition had created a kind of familiarity, and she had exercised her imagination until sometimes she suspected that she did *almost* remember and that real memory was hovering cruelly just out of reach on the very edge of her mind. She had rebuilt a quiet, conventional life round her family, but Connor was the true centre of her world. She loved her parents for their unquestioning support, loved Edward for his calm acceptance of her, but she adored her son with a fierce maternal joy and protectiveness that occasionally shook even her.

'There's something more up with you than Edward's sudden penny-pinching desire to regress and stay home with Mother,' Louise remarked with sudden insight.

The silence thickened. Faith reached a sudden decision and took a deep breath.

'A man spoke to me at the airport. He was very persistent. He insisted that he knew me by another name...Milly, he called me.' Trying to downplay the incident even now, Faith loosed an uneven laugh, but the pent-up words of strain continued to tumble from her. 'Maybe I have a *doppelgänger* somewhere. It was daft, but it was a little scary...'

'Why scary?'

Faith linked her hands tightly together in an effort to conceal their unsteadiness. 'You see, I noticed this man first...to be honest, I really couldn't take my eyes off him...' Her voice trailed away as embarrassment gripped her.

'So he was trying to make a move on you—but do tell me more,' Louise invited with amusement. 'Just why couldn't you take your eyes off this guy?'

'I don't know. He was very, very good-looking,' Faith conceded, colour flaming into her cheeks. 'And at first I thought that my staring at him had encouraged him to approach me. But when I thought about it afterwards... I don't think it was like that.'

'Why not? You might wear fuddy-duddy clothes and

scrape your hair back like a novice nun, but your kind of beauty would shine through a potato sack,' her friend advised her drily.

'This man was angry with me...I mean...with this woman, Milly,' Faith adjusted hurriedly. 'He accused her of having run away. And he was really astonished when I said I didn't know him and when I threatened him with the police.'

'That's persistent.' Louise looked more serious now.

'He said his name was Gianni D'Angelo...it means nothing to—'

Louise had straightened, an incredulous light in her eyes. 'Say that name again.'

'Gianni D'Angelo.'

'Did this guy ooze money?'

'He was very well dressed.'

'Gianni D'Angelo owns Macro Industries. He's a hugely important electronics mogul. My ex-hubby once worked on a major advertising campaign for one of his companies,' Louise informed her with dancing eyes. 'And if I thought a gorgeous single guy worth billions was wandering round Heathrow trying to pick up stray women, I'd take my sleeping bag and move in until he tripped over me!'

'It can't have been the same man,' Faith decided. 'I must've misheard the name.'

'Or perhaps you once enjoyed a champagne and caviar lifestyle, rubbing shoulders with the rich and the famous!' Louise teased with an appreciative giggle. 'I think you met a complete nutter stringing you a weird line, Faith.'

'Probably,' she agreed, with a noticeable diminution of tension.

With a sense of relief, Faith decided to put the entire silly episode out of her mind. And, just as she had arranged a couple of days earlier, she called in at the estate agent to collect the keys of the house which was her dream house for a second viewing.

True, Edward had not seen the sadly neglected Victorian

villa in quite the same light. But Faith knew she had to tell her fiancé why there was no question of her agreeing to move in with his widowed mother after their marriage. Perhaps then he would be more amenable to a property which needed a fair amount of work, she reasoned hopefully.

Set on the edge of town, in what had once been open countryside, the house rejoiced in a large garden screened from the road by tall hedges. Faith unlocked the front door and walked into the hall. The stale air made her wrinkle her nose, and she left the door wide on the weak morning sunlight. She wandered contentedly through the shabby rooms and finally into the old wooden conservatory which still possessed considerable charm. Edward had said it would have to be demolished.

A faint sound tugged Faith only partially from her cosy reverie. She half turned, without the slightest expectation of seeing anybody. So the shock of seeing Gianni D'Angelo ten feet away in the doorway was colossal. A strangled gasp escaped her convulsing throat, all colour draining from her face to highlight sapphire-blue eyes huge with fear.

'All I want to do is talk to you. I didn't want to walk into the shop. I didn't want to go to your home. At least here we're alone, on neutral territory.' He spread fluid brown hands in a soothing motion that utterly failed in its intent. 'I won't come any closer. I don't want to frighten you. I just want you to listen.'

But, in a state of petrified paralysis, Faith wasn't capable of listening. She started to shake, back away, her entire attention magnetically pinned to him, absorbing every aspect of his appearance in terrifyingly minute detail. His smoothly cropped but luxuriant black hair. His fabulous cheekbones. His classic nose. His perfectly modelled mouth. And the devastating strength of purpose dauntingly etched into every feature.

His charcoal-grey suit just screamed designer style and expense, moulding broad shoulders as straight as axe-

handles, accentuating the lithe flow of his lean, tightly mus-
cled all-male body. 'P-please…' she stammered sickly.

'*Per meraviglia!*' Gianni D'Angelo countered rawly.
'Since when were you a bag of nerves on the constant brink
of hysteria? All right, I'll just give you the proof that we
have had what you might call a prior acquaintance.'

'I don't want to have had a prior acquaintance with you!'
Faith exclaimed with stricken honesty. 'I want you to go
away and leave me alone!'

He withdrew something from the inside pocket of his
beautifully tailored jacket and extended it to her.

Faith stared, but wouldn't move forward to reach for the
item, which appeared to be a photograph.

'This is you just over three years ago,' he breathed in a
gritty undertone. 'And if you had your memory right now,
we'd be having a major fight.'

'A m-major fight…' Faith parroted weakly.

'I crept up on you with the camera. You were furious.
You made me promise to destroy the photo. I said I would.
I lied. I'm afraid it's the only photo of you I have left.'
Stooping with athletic ease, he tossed the glossy snap down
on the pitted tiled floor like a statement.

It skimmed to a halt about two feet from her. Faith stared
down at the snap where it lay. Her eyes opened impossibly
wide. She saw a slim, bare-breasted blonde semi-submerged
in bubbles in a giant bath. She saw a slim, bare-breasted
blonde with her face, her eyes, her mouth…her breasts. She
didn't want that brazen hussy to be her! Shock rolled over
her like a tidal wave.

'Keeping it was kind of a guy thing,' Gianni admitted,
almost roughly.

A strangled moan of denial slowly hissed from Faith's
rigidly compressed lips. Her head swam, the photo spinning
out of focus, her legs turning hollow. And then the great
well of darkness behind her eyelids sucked her down frighteningly fast into a faint.

Gianni caught her before she hit the floor in a crumpled
heap and swore vehemently.

hands it, screaming into the flow of his loud, nearly mus-
cled sot male body. Il pleasure and stammered stolidy.

Pat unrivaled. Gianni, D'Angelo bargained away
since then made you a basi of nerves on the coaster brink
of bwater. All the same, your love the proof that he
have and what you know and the acquaintance a-

CHAPTER TWO

FAITH drifted back to awareness in a complete daze. Her
lashes fluttered and then lifted. A dark male face swam into
stark focus, but it was those eyes, those stunning lion-gold
eyes fringed by black spiky lashes, that entrapped her attention and held her still. Her breath feathered in her throat.

The oddest little tugging sensation pulled deep down inside her, heralding a slow burst of heat that spread from the
pit of her stomach up, and then down to more intimate
places. Faith quivered in extreme disconcertion, extraordinarily conscious of the strange sensitivity of her full breasts,
the sudden straining tightness of her nipples. She couldn't
breathe, she couldn't speak, she couldn't think. Her body
had taken on a frightening life of its own, yet she couldn't
muster the power to either question or control it.

'Gianni…Gianni,' a breathless voice she barely recognised as her own pleaded achingly inside her mind.
Seemingly of its own volition, her hand lifted and began to
rise towards that strong, aggressive jawline…

Gianni's eyes shimmered chillingly. He broke the spell by
tilting his proud dark head back out of her reach. Then he
flashed her a look of raw derision. 'When I want sex, I'll
tell you, Milly. In the meantime, keep your hands to yourself.'

That assurance was so shattering it sprang Faith back to
full awareness. As he slid back upright from his crouching
position by the sagging basketwork chair on which she sat,
all that had happened in the minutes before she had fainted
flooded back to fill her with frantic, frightening confusion.

She had been viewing the house. He had arrived. He had
shown her the photo, that awful photo of herself flaunting

her bare breasts like a tart. He *did* know her. He *had* known her. Dear heaven, she conceded in drowning mortification, he had to have known her in the biblical sense. This man had actually slept with her.

Disorientation engulfed her. She heard afresh that pleading voice whispering his name inside her head, and wondered in stunned disbelief if after three long empty years she had *finally* remembered something from the past. Something she didn't want to remember, something that made her squirm with discomfiture. Perhaps it had been her imagination playing a trick on her. Why now and never before? She lifted her head and then suddenly dropped it down again, shutting her eyes tight, unable to meet Gianni D'Angelo's cool, measured gaze. A dulled throb of tension now pulsed behind her temples.

She recalled his derision, the blunt immediacy of what had been a rejection couched in the most humiliating terms. And then she relived what had prompted that crushing response from him. Oh, dear God, she thought with stunned shame, in those first moments of recovering consciousness she had focused on him and experienced the most unbelievably powerful surge of physical hunger. She was shattered by that realisation. It rewrote everything she had believed she knew about that side of her nature.

The sound of brisk footsteps sent her eyes flying open again. She gaped at the sight of the uniformed older man who appeared in the doorway to extend, of all things, a brandy goblet. Gianni took it from him with a nod and a dismissive move of one authoritative hand. He strode back to Faith and slotted the glass into her nerveless fingers. 'Drink it. You're as white as a sheet,' he instructed grimly.

'Wh-where did that man and this drink come from?' she stammered in unwilling wonderment.

Gianni frowned, as if that had been a very stupid question. 'When you passed out, I called my driver on the car phone and told him to bring it in.'

Faith slowly nodded, studying him with slightly glazed

eyes. Did he have a bar in his car? It had to be a big car. He wasn't giving her a bottle to swig out of. Her sense of dislocation from reality increased. The gulf between them felt immeasurable. According to Louise, Gianni D'Angelo was a very wealthy and powerful tycoon, and certainly he looked the part. What sort of relationship could she possibly have had with such a man? Suddenly she really didn't want to know.

'Drink the brandy,' Gianni pressed with controlled impatience.

'I hardly ever touch alcohol...'

'Well, you weren't on any wagon when I knew you,' Gianni informed her without hesitation.

Shaken by that come-back, and the daunting knowledge that was his alone, Faith tipped the glass to her lips. The spirit raced down her dry throat like liquid fire and burned away the chill spreading inside her. She swallowed hard and then breathed in deep. 'It seems you once knew me...I want that photograph back!' she added the instant she recalled its existence, anxious eyes lowering to see if it still lay on the floor. It didn't.

'Forget it; it's mine. But isn't that just like a woman?' Gianni growled with incredulous scorn. 'I only showed you that photo to make you accept that we once had a certain bond, and now you can only concentrate on a complete irrelevance!'

It didn't feel irrelevant to Faith. Right at that moment she saw that revealing photo as shocking evidence of a past she wanted to leave buried, and she certainly didn't want it left in his possession. 'Look, Mr D'Angelo—'

'*Mister* D'Angelo?' he queried, with a slashing smile that chilled her to the marrow. 'Make it Gianni.'

That ice-cold smile was like a threat. It shook her. He was poised several feet away, still as a predator about to spring. She recognised his hostility and recoiled from it in sudden fear. 'You hate me...'

He froze.

The silence thundered.

Suddenly he swung away from her. 'You don't remember me…you don't remember *anything*, do you?'

'No…I don't,' she conceded tautly.

'I thought you would've been full of questions. This isn't any easier for me,' he ground out in a charged undertone, spinning back to her with graceful but restive rapidity. Stormy dark eyes assailed her and she paled even more. 'At the airport, I admit I wanted to strangle you. I didn't know you'd lost your memory. I don't like you looking at me like I'm about to attack you either!'

Intimidated by the powerful personality that he was revealing, Faith did nothing to soothe him when she instinctively cowered back into the chair.

'Milly…'

'That's not my name!' she protested.

He let that go past.

'Look…' He spread the fingers of one lean and eloquent hand. 'You're scared because I'm rocking your cosy little world. It's not me you're afraid of. You're scared of the unknown that I represent.'

Faith gave a slight wary nod that might or might not have signified agreement, but her expressive eyes revealed her surprise that he could make that distinction. She wasn't used to the sensation of someone else trying to get inside her head and work out how she felt.

'I don't want to frighten you, but anything I tell you is likely to cause you distress, so I'll keep it basic.'

'How did you find out where I was living? How did you know I was an amnesiac?' Faith suddenly demanded accusingly.

'Naturally I had you followed from the airport. Then I had some enquiries made,' Gianni supplied with a fluid shrug.

Rising in one sudden motion from the chair, Faith gave him a stricken look of bemusement. 'But why would you do something like that? Why would you go to so much trouble? Why are you here now? Just because we had some relationship years ago?'

'I'm working up to that. I did have this rather naïve hope that you might start remembering things when you saw me again,' Gianni confided with a sardonic laugh, his smooth, dark features broodingly taut. 'But it looks like I'm going to have to do this the hard way. I suggest you sit down again.'

'No.' Faith braced her slim shoulders, a sudden powerful need to regain control of the situation driving her. 'I don't need to put myself through this if I don't want to. I don't need to listen to you—'

Gianni murmured, 'I'm afraid you do...'

'No, I don't. I just want you to go away and leave me alone,' Faith admitted truthfully, suppressing the little inner voice that warned her that that was craven and short-sighted. For here it finally was, the opportunity she had once yearned for: the chance to knock a window, however small, into that terrible wall that closed her out from her own memory. Yet because she didn't know, indeed strongly feared what she might glimpse through that window, she was rejecting the chance.

Gianni D'Angelo surveyed her with disturbing intensity, brilliant eyes semi-screened by his lush lashes to a glimmer of gold. 'That's not possible. You asked me why I was here. So I'll tell you. It's quite simple. When you disappeared out of my life, you were pregnant with my child...'

A roaring sounded in Faith's ears. Her lips parted. She stared back at him in horror as that cosy little world he had referred to with such perceptible scorn lurched and tilted dangerously on its axis.

'Connor is *my* son,' Gianni spelt out levelly.

The very floor under Faith's feet seemed to shift. Her eyes were blank with shock.

As she swayed, Gianni strode forward. Curving a powerful arm to her spine to steady her, he took her out of the conservatory and back through the hall. 'No, don't pass out on me again. Let's get out of this dump. We both need some fresh air.'

The winter sunlight that engulfed her at the front of the house seemed impossibly bright. She blinked and shifted her aching head. 'No, not Connor…it's not possible…not *you*!'

Ignoring those objections, Gianni guided her over to a worn bench and settled her down on it with surprisingly gentle hands. He hunkered down in front of her and reached for her trembling fingers, enclosing them firmly in his. 'There *is* no easy way to tell you these things. I'm working really hard to keep the shocks to the minimum.'

That one shock had temporarily left her bereft of the ability to even respond. And yet he could call that one bombshell keeping the shocks to the ''minimum''? Dear God, what worse could he tell her than he had already told her? Her face was pale as parchment. 'My head hurts,' she mumbled, like a child seeking sympathy in an effort to ward off punishment for some offence.

Gianni's hands tightened fiercely on hers. 'I'm sorry, but I had to tell you. Why do you think I'm here? Why do you think I've spent three endless years trying to trace you both?' he demanded emotively.

Faith focused on him numbly. The father of her child. Why hadn't that possibility occurred to her sooner? But she knew why, didn't she? Connor might as well have sprung into being without benefit of any male input whatsoever.

Once she had been frantic to know who had fathered her child, but when she had admitted that need to her parents they had gone all quiet and looked at each other uncomfortably. And when she had questioned their attitude to what seemed to her an absolutely crucial question that had to be answered, she had recognised what they didn't want to put into words.

They were afraid that she had been promiscuous, that she might not even know for sure who had actually got her pregnant. And she had been very upset to realise that her parents could harbour such sordid suspicions about a life she could no longer remember.

'The father of my baby might love me...might be looking for me right now!' she had sobbed in distraught self-defence.

'If he loved you, why were you on your own?'

'If you disappeared, why hasn't he been in touch with the police?'

'And why hasn't he come here looking for you? Surely he would at least have known where your parents lived? Even though you hadn't been in touch with us recently, wouldn't he have arrived here to check us out as a last re-sort?'

Faced with those unanswerable questions, Faith had fi-nally let go of the idea that she might have conceived her baby in a caring relationship. And from that moment on she had begun suppressing her own curiosity, shrinking from the idea that Connor might be the result of some casual sexual encounter. Yet those suspicions had only fronted worse fears, she conceded now, a hysterical laugh lodging like a giant stone in her throat. These days you read so many hor-ror stories about the level penniless and homeless teenagers could be reduced to just to survive...

'Milly...' Gianni tugged her upright.

'That's n-not my name,' she stated through chattering teeth.

He raised his hands to capture her taut cheekbones and she shivered because he was so very close. 'That's the name I knew you by,' he murmured softly.

'Please let go of me...'

'You're shaking like a jerry-built building in an earth-quake,' Gianni countered drily.

She realised that she was. Involuntarily, she braced her hands on his chest. Instantly the heat of him sprang out at her and she swiftly removed her hands again, almost off-balancing in her eagerness to put some distance between them. But the distinctive scent of him still flared in her nos-trils. Clean, warm, intrinsically male and somehow earthy in a way Edward was not. Edward always smelt of soap. *Oh, my God, Edward,* a voice screamed inside her pounding head.

Another moan was dredged from her. She covered her distraught face with trembling hands in growing desperation. Connor, whom she loved beyond life itself. Connor's father was here to stake a claim in his son's life. What else could he be here for? Why else had he searched for them?

'Let me tell you something…' Gianni breathed in a charged undertone that reeked of menace but somehow didn't frighten her. 'Three years without me has turned you into a basket case! I'm taking you back to my hotel and getting a doctor to look you over!'

By sheer force of will he got her down the path and out onto the pavement. She wasn't capable of matching the speed of his reactions, but she dimly registered that what he thought he acted on simultaneously, with terrifying decisiveness. She gawped at the sight of the long silver limousine waiting, not to mention the chauffeur surging round the bonnet as if he was running a race to get the passenger door open in time.

'Your hotel…?' she repeated belatedly, her brain functioning only in tiny, cripplingly slow bursts of activity. 'I can't go to your *hotel*!'

Gianni ducked her head down as carefully as an officer of the law tucking a suspect into a police car and settled her onto the rich leather-backed seat. He swung in beside her, forcing her to move deeper into the opulent car, and a split second later the door slammed on them both.

'I'm not going anywhere with you!' Faith protested frantically. 'I've got to get back to the shop—'

'I'm sure your partner will manage without you for a couple of hours.'

'I have to pick up Connor from the nursery…no, I don't…I *forgot*,' she lied jerkily. 'The kids are out on a trip today and they won't be back until—'

Gianni subjected her to a derisive appraisal. 'Wise up,' he

breathed in cool interruption. 'You can't hide Connor or keep him from me. When I want to meet my son, I will, but I'm unlikely to stage that meeting when you're on the edge of hysteria.'

He had seen right through her, and that terrified her. 'I'm not on the edge of hysteria...my car...the house...it wasn't locked up—'

Gianni held up the keys. 'I pulled the door shut behind us. If you give me your car keys, your car will be picked up and driven over to the hotel. You're in no condition to drive.'

Faith surveyed him with huge haunted eyes. She passed over her car keys. He was like a tank, rolling over her to crush her deeper and deeper into the dust. And so cold, so very, very cold, she sensed with a shiver. He had tried to calm her, gripped her hands, made an effort to show that he understood why she was so distressed. But none of that had worked. Why? There was no human warmth in him. His brilliant, beautiful dark eyes now chilled her to ice.

Connor's eyes were lighter in shade, but his skin always had that same golden tint even in winter, she reflected numbly. Maybe he was lying about Connor being his child! Even as her head pounded unmercifully into what felt like the onset of a migraine attack she discarded that faint hope. Gianni D'Angelo wouldn't be wasting his time tracking down a child he didn't know to be his.

Stray, unconnected thoughts kept on hitting her from all directions. She had shared his bed. She shifted on the seat, totally unable to look at him any more. She had bathed in his bath. It had to have been *his* bath. Nothing would convince her that she had ever been in the bracket of owning so luxurious a bath. But he had avoided the usual word 'relationship' to describe their former intimacy. 'A certain bond'. That was the phrase he had used. Such an odd choice to describe their...their what?

Not an affair, not a relationship? Oh, dear heaven, had she been a one-night stand? Or worse? And she knew what was worse. No, no. She discarded that melodramatic suspicion. If she'd been a hooker, he would hardly be so sure her son was his. Dear heaven, what was she thinking? It was as if her brain had just been unhinged, torn open to let all her most deep-seated anxieties flood out.

In silence, Gianni reached into the built-in bar and withdrew a glass. He poured another brandy and settled it meaningfully into her trembling fingers.

Had she drunk a lot when he knew her? Been a real boozer with a strong head? She raised the glass to her lips, the rim rattling against her teeth. The nightmare just went on and on. What did he want from her? She was too terrified to ask, was in a state of complete panic, incapable of rational dialogue.

She didn't even notice where the limo had been going until he helped her out of the car. It was a big country house hotel about three miles out of town. Faith had dined there on her twenty-sixth birthday. Even her father, who liked to make a show of sophistication, had winced at the cost of that meal.

'I don't want to go in here…just take me home,' she mumbled. 'I'm not feeling very well.'

'You can lie down for a while,' Gianni assured her. 'Get your head together.'

'You're not listening to me—'

'You're not saying anything I want to hear.'

'Did I ever?' she heard herself whisper as he pressed her into the lift and the doors slid shut on them.

His superb bone structure tautened. 'I don't remember,' he said flatly.

Her tummy twisted. Was he making fun of her?

Gianni stared down at her from his imposing height. His mouth curled. 'I guess you could say I don't *want* to remember. It's irrelevant now.'

Her head felt woozy, her legs weak and wobbly. As the lift disgorged them into a smoothly carpeted reception area containing only one door, he settled a bracing hand on her spine. 'I don't want to be here,' she told him afresh.

'I know, but I have a habit of getting what I want.' He made her precede him into an incredibly spacious and luxurious suite. Closing the door, he bent, and without the slightest hesitation scooped her off her feet.

'What are you doing?' she gasped.

'You should've said no to that second drink. But possibly I did you a favour. The alcohol has acted on you like a tranquilliser.' Thrusting open another door, he crossed the room beyond and laid her down on a big bed. 'The doctor will check you out in a few minutes. I brought him down from London with me.'

'I don't need a doctor.'

Gianni studied her without any expression at all and strode back out of the room, leaving the door slightly ajar.

A doctor did come. He was middle-aged and suave. If he gave her his name, she didn't catch it. She was finding it impossible to concentrate, and she was so tired, so unbelievably tired, it took almost incalculable effort to respond to his questions...

Gianni watched Milly sleep. Grudging pity stirred in him. She looked so fragile, and it wasn't an illusion. Right now, Milly was like a delicate porcelain cup with a hair-fine crack. If he wasn't very careful, she would break in half, and he might never get her glued back together again. Connor needed his mother. Connor did not need a mother having a nervous breakdown over the identity crisis that was soon to engulf her.

Porca miseria, Gianni swore inwardly. He wanted to wipe Robin and Davina Jennings from the face of the earth for screwing Milly up. She wasn't the same person any more. She was a shadow imprint. Anxious, nervous as a cat, apologetic, scared. She didn't know him from Adam and yet she had just let him bring her back to his hotel suite. In her current condition she was as foolishly trusting as a very young child.

But there was nothing immature about Gianni's response to her. He wanted to rip her out of that buttoned-up white blouse and gathered floral skirt she wore and free her glorious hair from that ugly plait. And then he wanted to jump her like an animal and keep her in bed for at least twenty-four hours, he acknowledged, with grim acceptance of his own predictability.

He had really hoped she would leave him cold. But she didn't. Sooner or later she would. She was a woman, like other women, and eventually all women bored him. Only she never had in the past, he conceded reluctantly. And if he hadn't caught her with Stefano he would have married her. His dirt-poor Sicilian background of traditional values had surfaced when he'd got her pregnant. He had been ready to buy into the whole dream. The wife, the child, the family hearth. And this tiny, fragile woman, who would only reach his heart now if she stood on literal tiptoes, had exploded the dream and destroyed his relationship with his brother.

He had wanted revenge so badly he could still taste it even now. He had come down to Oxfordshire intending to let revenge simply take its natural course. He emitted a humourless laugh. He hated her, but he craved the oblivion of her sweet body like a drug addict craved a fix. He hated her, but he couldn't bring himself to hurt her. He hated the Jenningses for making him the weapon that had to hurt. He had no choice but to blow Milly's cosy little fake world away. She had to take her own life back, and she couldn't do that without him...

A slight, slanting smile eased the ferocious tension stamped on Gianni's features. She was *his*. He cursed the rampant stirring in his loins. He had been in a state of near constant arousal ever since the airport. Only rigid self-discipline and cold intellect restrained him. For the foreseeable future, she was untouchable. He had waited three years; he could wait a little longer. The fiancé had to be seen off.

How *was* Mr Square and Upwardly Mobile likely to react to the news that Milly wasn't really the boss's daughter?

Milly shifted in her sleep and turned over. The plait lay temptingly exposed on the pillow. Gianni moved forward, and before he even knew what he was doing he was unclasping the stiff black bow, loosening the strands, running his long fingers through her beautiful silky hair. His hands weren't quite steady. Instantly he withdrew them, studied them broodingly, clenched them into defensive fists.

When she had her memory back and he had enjoyed her for a while, he would dump her again. But he would retain a lot of visiting privileges. Purely for his son's benefit, of course. The cascade of half-unravelled wavy golden hair hung over the side of the bed like a lethal lure. It might be quite a while until he dumped her. So what? He asked himself. You couldn't put a price on pleasure.

But how did he tell her the truth about herself in a way that didn't make her hate him? How did you wrap up the fact that at heart she was a gold-digging, cheating tramp who had fooled him right to the bitter end? And if she got her memory back she was going to remember that she had run rings round him right from the minute she'd jumped out of that birthday cake. She was his one weakness, but he could afford to indulge himself just one more time. As long as he never let himself forget for a second what she was *really* like…

'Angel…?'

Somebody was shaking her awake. Faith began to sit up, opening her eyes, only to freeze into immobility.

Gianni D'Angelo stood over her. So very tall, so exotically dark.

'What did you call me?' she mumbled, remembering everything, attempting to block it back out again until she felt better equipped to deal with it.

Faint colour scored his hard cheekbones. 'Milly…I called you Milly.'

'My name's Faith,' she told him flatly, refusing to consider his assurance that he had known her by that other name because such an astonishing claim raised questions about her past she could not yet bring herself to ask. 'Why on earth did you bring me here?'

'You needed time out.'

With a sudden start of dismay, Faith checked her watch. It was almost one. She began to scramble off the bed with alacrity. 'I need to pick up Connor—'

'Call Mrs Jennings. You should eat before you get back behind a steering wheel.'

Mrs Jennings? What an odd way to refer to her mother! Struggling to regain her equilibrium, Faith was even more disconcerted by the untidy cascade of hair now falling round her face. The clasp must have fallen off while she slept. Thrusting the waving mass back behind one small ear, she frowned in Gianni's general direction. 'Eat? I have to pick up Connor—'

He extended a mobile phone to her. 'Ask Mrs Jennings to do it today. We need to talk.'

'No, I—'

'You can't run away from this.'

You can't run away from this. That blunt statement unnerved her. Her lower lip trembled, and then firmed. She twisted her golden head away and snatched in a shuddering breath. Once again Gianni D'Angelo had seen right through her. Her parents and Edward had always been content to accept what they saw on the surface.

And how *was* her fiancé likely to react to the sudden appearance of Connor's natural father? Badly—probably very badly, Faith acknowledged dully. Edward was a very conservative man. And he had once admitted that the very fact he was the only man involved in Connor's life had made it easier for him to accept her son.

The mobile phone was pressed into her tense fingers.

'You think you can just tell me what to do—' she began accusingly.

'Right now, you'd seize on any excuse to walk out of here again!'

Reddening at the accuracy of that stab, Faith turned back reluctantly to look at Gianni D'Angelo.

And, like a slap in the face, she saw all the cool control she craved etched into the arrogant angle of his dark head and the steadiness of his burnished dark gaze. He had complete dominion over himself.

'When you've made your call, we'll have lunch.'

Her teeth ground together. She couldn't hold back her hostility any longer. 'I really don't like you.'

Gianni stilled with one brown hand on the door. 'I know... The Sleeping Beauty woke up to a kiss—'

'She also woke up to a prince!' Faith heard herself interrupt, and then she stiffened, disturbed by the speed of her own retaliation. She never argued with anybody. She was far better known as a peacemaker.

'If I'd kissed you, you might have screamed assault...although possibly that's only what you'd prefer me to believe.' Gianni surveyed her, a sardonic slant to his expressive mouth. 'I think your body remembers me better than your brain does.'

Faith was aghast at that suggestion. 'How *dare* you?'

Gianni gave an exaggerated wince. 'Tell me, how do you square the outraged prudish virgin act with the reality that you're a single mother?'

Beneath his coolly enquiring gaze, Faith's soft mouth opened and closed again. Colour flooded her complexion.

'When something irritates the hell out of me, I usually mention it,' Gianni shared, before he turned on his heel and left her alone.

In his wake, a combustible mix of anger and chagrin engulfed Faith. She punched out her home phone number with a stabbing finger. Her mother answered.

'It's Faith. I'm sorry, but I won't be home for lunch...and I hate to ask you at such short notice but could you pick up Connor from nursery for me?' Faith asked tautly.

'Of course I can, darling,' Davina Jennings responded instantly. 'You sound flustered. Is the shop very busy or is Louise away? Never mind. I'd better get a move on if I'm to collect my grandson *and* still have lunch ready for your father!'

'Thanks, Mum.'

Faith laid down the mobile. As she did so she caught a glimpse of herself in a mirror. *Outraged virgin?* Her cheeks burned afresh. Was that really how she came across?

During her convalescence her mother had warned her that she had a reputation to rebuild, that folk would be quick to pass final judgement on an unmarried mother. Already the target of considerable local curiosity, Faith had been painfully aware of her parents' concern about how she might behave. Her parents were very private people, but they were pillars of both church and community. So Faith had followed her mother's guidance when it came to her wardrobe and had worked hard at cultivating an acceptably low profile.

Distractedly, Faith lifted one of the silver brushes on the dresser to try and tidy her hair as she couldn't find her clasp anywhere. There had been nothing prudish about that blonde in the bath…and, whether she liked it or not, that blonde *had* been her! Yet she still found that so hugely hard to accept. It was like the sudden discovery of an identical twin, who was her exact opposite in personality and behaviour.

After all, in three long years Faith had never had the slightest urge to go to bed with anybody! Quite a few men had asked her out. Unfortunately most had had definite expectations of how the evening should end. Repulsed by those pushy advances, Faith had come to believe that she had a pretty low sex drive, and had occasionally marvelled at Connor's very existence.

Edward had been a family friend long before they had started seeing each other, and she had been grateful that he seemed so ideally suited to her. Her fiancé was neither physically demonstrative nor sexually demanding. He had informed her that he preferred to save intimacy for marriage.

He had even told her that he would respect her more on those terms, particularly when she had made what he called 'a youthful mistake'. When it had dawned on her that the 'mistake' Edward was referring to was Connor, she had been mortified and hurt.

When Faith walked back into the beautifully furnished reception room next door, she saw a waiter standing by a trolley in the elegant dining area. Gianni was poised by the window. He watched her approach with unfathomable eyes. Her tummy flipped and her breathing quickened.

'Let's eat,' he suggested smoothly.

She was surprised to discover how hungry she was, and was grateful for the restraining presence of the waiter. Gianni embarked on an impersonal conversation. He questioned her about local businesses and the recent bankruptcies on the industrial estate. His razor-sharp intellect swiftly outran the depths of her economic knowledge. Where another man might have centred his interest on local history, or the sights to be seen, Gianni functioned on an entirely different level.

Involuntarily, Faith was fascinated. In the midst of her nightmare, Gianni D'Angelo could behave as if nothing remotely abnormal was happening. It was intimidating proof of a very resourceful and clever male in absolute control of a difficult situation.

When the waiter departed after serving them, Faith tensed up again. Gianni surveyed her with slumbrous dark golden eyes and her throat tightened, her heartbeat speeding up.

'Now it's time to talk about Connor,' he told her with immovable cool.

'Connor? How can we?' Faith protested without hesitation. 'As it is, I can hardly get my mind around the idea that you *could* be his father!'

'Not could be, *am*,' Gianni countered with level emphasis. 'You had a test shortly before your disappearance for the child's DNA. I am, without a single shadow of a doubt, Connor's father.'

Faith's knife and fork fell from her loosening hold to rattle jarringly down on her plate. She stared back at him, appalled by that revealing admission. 'You weren't sure that…well, that… You mean you didn't trust me…you suspected there might've been room for doubt?' She struggled valiantly to frame that horribly humiliating question, and her strained voice shook.

Gianni's lean, dark devastating face was now as still as a woodland pool. He cursed his error in referring to the DNA tests to convince her that Connor was his son and murmured evenly, 'I'm a very rich man. The DNA testing was a necessary precaution.'

'A n-necessary precaution…?' Faith stammered.

'A legal safeguard,' Gianni extended with a slight shift of one broad shoulder. 'Once Connor was proven to be my child I could be sure that if anything happened to me his inheritance rights would not be easily contested.'

Faith nodded uncertainly, thoroughly taken aback by the obvious fact that Gianni D'Angelo had already thought to make provision for her son in his will. She also registered that she herself had already moved on in terms of acceptance and expectation. Only three hours ago she had wanted Gianni to vanish, had denied any need to know what ties they might once have had. But now she badly needed to be reassured that they had had a stable relationship which would *not* have entailed DNA testing simply to confirm the paternity of her child.

'You said I was trying to run away from all this,' she reminded him tautly, her clear blue eyes pinned anxiously to his hard bronzed features. 'At first, yes, I was. I was so shocked. But now I have a whole lot of questions I need to ask.'

'About us,' Gianni slotted in softly. 'Unfortunately it would be a bad idea for me to unload too many facts on you right now.'

Faith frowned in complete confusion. 'Why?'

His stunning eyes veiling, Gianni pushed away his plate

and lounged back fluidly in his chair to study her. 'I talked
to a psychologist before I came down here.'

'A psychologist?' Disconcerted pink surged up beneath
her skin at that admission. The embarrassed distaste with
which her parents had regarded all such personnel had left
its mark on her.

'It was his view that wherever possible you should only
be expected to deal with one thing at a time. That's why
we're concentrating on Connor,' Gianni explained, with the
slow quiet diction of someone dealing with a child on the
brink of a tantrum. 'At this moment, that's enough for you
to handle.'

'Let me get this straight,' Faith muttered unevenly. 'You
are telling me that you are not prepared to—'

'Muddy the water and confuse you with what is currently
extraneous information,' Gianni confirmed, watching her
eyes darken and flare with incredulous anger.

Abruptly thrusting back her chair, Faith rose to her feet.
'Who the heck do you think you are to tell me that?'

'Sit down and finish your meal,' Gianni drawled.

Faith trembled. 'I have the right to know what role I
played in your life. That is *not* extraneous information!'

'I think it is. I want to talk about my son because I've
waited three years to find him and now I would very much
like to meet him.' Gianni's measured gaze challenged her.

'You're not meeting Connor until you tell me what I need
to know!' Faith's head was starting to pound, not least because a temper she had never known she had was tightening
its grip on her, no matter how hard she strove to contain it.
'What was I to you? A one-night stand? *A hooker?*' she
slung furiously. 'Or a girlfriend?'

With pronounced cool, Gianni came upright to face her.
Even in the overwrought state she was in, his striking grace
of movement caught her eye as he stepped out from behind
the table. 'No to all of the above. Leave this for another day,
cara,' he advised very quietly, incisive dark-as-night eyes
resting on the revealing clenching and unclenching of her

hands. 'When the time's right, I'll tell you everything you want to know.'

'Stop treating me like I'm mentally unfit to deal with my *own* life!' Faith launched back at him in furious condemnation. 'I'll ask you one more time before I walk out of here...what was I to you?'

Gianni expelled his breath in a slow hiss. 'You were my mistress.'

Faith stared back at him, eyes widening and widening, soft mouth rounding but no sound emerging. The angry tension evaporated from her. Sheer shock stilled her, leaving her looking vulnerable and lost. Then she sealed her lips, forced her feet to turn her around and walked to the door. There she hesitated, wheeled back, and hurried across the room again to retrieve her handbag. Not once did she allow her attention to roam back in Gianni's direction.

'Are my car keys in here?' she asked woodenly.

'Yes. This is ridiculous,' Gianni murmured drily.

'How long was I...your mistress?' Faith squeezed out that designation as if her mouth was a clothes-wringer.

'Two years...'

Faith flinched as though he had struck her a second body blow. Then, pushing up her chin and straightening her slight shoulders, she moved back to the door and paused there. 'I hope you paid me well to prostitute myself,' she breathed through painfully compressed lips.

In the thunderous silence that greeted that stinging retaliation Faith turned her head. Gianni gazed back at her, not a muscle moving on his darkly handsome features. But for once she could read him like an open book. His golden eyes blazed his fury. Oddly soothed by that reaction, Faith stalked rigid-backed out of the suite and headed for the lift.

CHAPTER THREE

FAITH'S tenuous control crumpled and fell apart the instant she reached the sanctuary of her car.

Snatching in a gasping breath in an effort to calm herself, Faith stared blindly through the windscreen. *His mistress!* It made a horrible kind of sense. He was filthy rich. She wasn't from the same world. So of course she hadn't been his girl-friend, his *equal*, she reflected bitterly. Now she knew why he had been challenged to quantify their relationship. The commercial element had figured. For two years. *Two years*, an agonised inner voice screeched in condemnation. It had taken her an inexcusably long time to wake up and see the error of her ways.

For two years, two of her missing years, she had been a kept woman. In exchange for sex he had probably paid for the roof over her head, her clothing, all her bills. Faith shud-dered, mortified by the self she had clearly been before she'd lost her memory. What kind of woman could she have been? This woman who had called herself Milly? What further humiliating discoveries still awaited her?

Striving hard to get a grip on her wildly seesawing emo-tions, Faith started the car and drove away from the hotel. Gianni had said she had disappeared. OK, she told herself, it might have taken her a long time but at least she had finally decided to leave him. She must have planned to make a fresh start. And a fresh start was exactly what she had made, she reminded herself doggedly.

Then, just as she came off the roundabout on the outskirts of town, her searing headache became suddenly so much worse that her vision began to blur. Immediately she pulled off the road and parked. Perspiration beaded her short upper lip.

And then it happened. As if somebody was staging a sudden slideshow inside her head. A picture slotted into her mind. She saw herself clutching a phone like a lifeline, and then her awareness shifted and she was suddenly inside that self.

'Gianni...I haven't seen you in three weeks,' she was saying, and tears were stinging her eyes, but she was working really hard at keeping her voice light and teasing because like any workaholic Gianni hated it when she nagged.

'Book yourself a seat on Concorde.'

'OK...' she agreed with studied casualness, furiously blinking back the tears.

'I didn't realise it had been three weeks.' Gianni paused, and then continued with innate superiority and instinctive attention to detail. 'No, it hasn't been three weeks, *cara*. Don't you remember I stopped over one night before I went to Rio?'

'Gianni, much as I love you,' she groaned, 'there are times when I just want to reach down this phone line and *hit* you! You were here for less than five hours!'

And then, just as quickly as it had come, the picture vanished and Faith was left sitting behind the steering wheel of her car in complete shock. But every emotion she had experienced during that slide back into the past had stayed with her, and the revelation of those powerful emotions now took her by storm.

Winding down the window with a shaking hand, Faith drank in great gulps of fresh air. It had happened, this time it had really, definitely happened, and she had genuinely remembered something. But that tiny slice of the past she had relived had been incredibly disturbing.

She had loved him. She had *loved* Gianni D'Angelo! She had had a capacity for emotion then that had virtually eaten her alive. Until now Faith had never dreamt that at any stage of her life she could have experienced such strong feelings.

And it was even more devastating to be forced to accept that once she had adored Gianni D'Angelo, lived from one day to the next on that love, needed him as she needed air to breathe, felt she was barely existing when he wasn't around...

Emerging from that shattering new awareness, Faith tried to block it out again. It had already been a hell of a day. Tomorrow she would take it all out again and deal with it. Not now.

She drove through town and parked at the rear of Petals, the flowershop she ran with Louise.

Gianni D'Angelo's mistress. If she had once been *that* crazy about him, she could even begin to see how she might have ended up trapped in such a relationship. Love had made a fool of her. Love, she told herself urgently, was a lot more presentable an excuse than avarice.

But how was she to tell Edward? Edward was such a conventional man. Faith's heart sank. Edward had chosen to assume that some flash young man had seduced her and then abandoned her when she fell pregnant. That was how Edward had dealt with getting engaged to an unwed mother. He had effectively excused her from all real responsibility and decided to view her as an innocent victim.

But being kept by Gianni D'Angelo as a mistress was a very different kettle of fish. And how could she not tell Edward, when Gianni was here in the flesh demanding to meet his son? It was *all* going to come out. Nothing she could do could prevent that. Gianni D'Angelo's mistress. It was sordid. Why had she tried briefly to persuade herself otherwise? Edward and her parents would be extremely shocked. And Gianni wasn't likely to sink back into the woodwork again. Climbing out of her car, Faith paled at that awareness.

The shop was empty of customers. Louise was dusting shelves and humming to herself. Her partner turned round, and as Faith moved into the light she frowned. 'Heck, what's happened to you?'

Faith stiffened defensively like a hedgehog under sudden attack. 'Nothing...nothing's happened to me.'

'What have you done with your hair?' Louise demanded. 'My goodness, I never realised you had that much of it!'

'I had a headache...have a headache,' Faith corrected awkwardly. 'I'm sorry. I should've called you to tell you that I would be out for so long.'

'Nonsense. Go back home this minute. You look awful,' Louise told her bluntly.

Relieved by that advice, Faith went back out to her car and drove slowly home to the rambling old farmhouse her parents had bought and renovated when she was a child. In the cosy front hall, the scent of beeswax polish and the ticking of the old grandfather clock enveloped her like a healing blanket.

Connor ran out of the kitchen, loosed a noisy whoop of welcome and flung himself at her. 'Mummy!' he carolled.

Faith reached down and lifted her son. She hugged him so tightly he gave a yelp of protest. Instantly she loosened her grip and pressed an apologetic kiss to his smooth brow. A great gush of love had just engulfed her, but for the first time there was a piercing arrow of fearful insecurity inside that love.

He was a gorgeous little boy. The combination of her blonde hair with his dark brows, sparkling brown eyes and golden skin tone was unusual. But all of a sudden Connor wasn't exclusively her little boy any more. He was the son of a very rich man, who wanted a share of him. How much of a share?

Her mother emerged from the kitchen. 'Are you taking the rest of the afternoon off?' she asked, and then frowned. 'Oh dear, what's happened to your hair?'

'I lost the clasp.'

Davina Jennings, a small, comfortably rounded woman with short greying fair hair and an air of bustling activity, sighed. 'You should take time off more often. You do look tired, darling.'

'Do I?'' Averting her head, Faith lowered Connor to the floor.

She would talk to her parents tonight after dinner. There was no point putting it off. Gianni might just arrive on the doorstep. Possibly storming out on him hadn't been the wisest move. It might have made her feel better but it would have increased his hostility. And how could she blame *him* for the reality that she had been his mistress? She had been an adult when she had made that choice, not a helpless little girl.

'Since you're home, I think I'll just pop down to the church hall and check that everything's ready for that choral do this evening,' Davina Jennings continued. 'I know Janet Markham said she would see to it, but I'm afraid the younger women on the ladies' committee aren't always as reliable as they like to think.'

Faith knew that her mother would be out for the rest of the afternoon. Davina loved to be busy. She would go down to the church hall, seize with alacrity on the idea that the floor wasn't quite clean enough or the kitchen looked a little dingy and roll up her sleeves.

Faith went upstairs to her bedroom. Connor got down on his knees to run a toy car along the skirting board, making phroom-phroom noises while she got changed. She pulled on a sweater and a comfy denim skirt and took Connor out to the garden.

It was a lovely mild winter day. But the sense of tranquillity that usually enveloped her outdoors refused to come. What would Gianni do next? She was just sitting here on pins waiting to find out, wasn't she? Suddenly ashamed of her own passiveness, Faith walked into the kitchen and reached for the phone. It made sense that she should contact Gianni to arrange to meet up with him. The last thing she wanted was for him to arrive unannounced at her home...

But the receptionist at the hotel didn't seem to know whether they had a Gianni D'Angelo staying or not. Yet she still requested Faith's name and address before she might condescend to pass on such privileged information. Exasperated, because she was afraid she might lose her nerve, Faith decided to leave a message instead.

'Tell him Milly would like to see him. I'll be...I'll be in the park at four,' she dictated tautly, and hurriedly replaced the receiver.

Cloak and dagger stuff, but why give her own name when it wasn't necessary? And this way she would get the worst over with, she told herself bracingly. She would let him see Connor and find out exactly what he wanted. She was dealing with a very rich and powerful male, who was already hostile towards her. At this point, antagonising him without good reason would be foolish.

An hour later, Faith drew into the car park. There was no limo, so Gianni hadn't arrived yet. In fact there were no other cars parked at all. With Connor holding her hand, Faith walked down the sloping path that ran between the steeply banked wildflower meadows towards the playground and the artificial lake. Her heart was now beating so fast she pressed a hand against her breast.

She rounded a corner and saw a man in a dark suit talking into a radio. She tensed, wondering what he was doing, suddenly appreciating that she had come to a very lonely place at an hour when it was likely to be deserted. The man fell silent as she moved past. Connor pulled free of her hold and ran ahead into the playground, his sturdy little legs carrying him towards the slide he loved at a steady rate of knots.

'See me, Mummy!' he shouted breathlessly as he reached the final step, his face ablaze with achievement.

And at that exact moment Gianni appeared, striding down the path she had just emerged from. Something disturbingly akin to excitement flashed through Faith, freezing her in her tracks. The man with the radio spoke to him, but Gianni slashed a silencing hand through the air. Gianni's entire attention was already fixed on the little boy carefully settling himself to the top of the slide, tiny hands holding the toddler grips tight.

The whole atmosphere seemed to charge up. Faith couldn't take her eyes off Gianni. She watched him swallow, slowly shake his gleaming dark head in an almost vulnerable movement, and suddenly ram his hands into the pockets of his exquisitely tailored trousers. He stared at Connor as if he was the Holy Grail, and he did it with a raw intensity of emotional response that shook Faith to her innermost depths.

Did he ever look at *me* like that? she found herself wondering. She wouldn't have credited that Gianni D'Angelo had that much emotion in him. But the stark prominence of his superb bone structure, the shimmering brilliance of his ferociously intent eyes and the hands that he didn't seem to know what to do with any more as he jerked them back out of his pockets again all spoke for him.

Her throat thickened. Suddenly she felt on the outside, looking in. She had picked a guy who loved children but she had run away with his child. Why had she done that? He had known she was pregnant before she left him. Why *had* she left him? Hadn't she realised that he might feel like this about their baby?

Without the slightest warning or expectation, Faith was beginning to feel guilty.

He had known her by another name. Clearly she had lied to him and given him that false name. Why had she done that? Had she been ashamed of the life she was leading with him? Had she been trying to ensure that nobody could ever connect Faith Jennings with Gianni D'Angelo's mistress? Well, her lies must have hampered his every attempt to find them again. He couldn't possibly have known where her parents lived, or indeed anything about them.

'Whee!' Connor screeched as he whooshed down the slide, scrambling off at the foot to race back round to the steps to do it again, totally uninterested in the adults watching him.

'He's blond...' Gianni breathed gruffly from his stance several feet away, still not sparing her an actual glance. 'Somehow I never thought of that.'

Faith's breath feathered in her tightening throat. 'He has dark eyes and dark brows and he takes a tremendous tan,' she squeezed out unevenly. 'And he's pretty tall for his age, which he certainly didn't get from me—'

'He's just tremendous,' Gianni incised almost roughly, his foreign accent far more noticeable than it had been earlier in the day.

One day, in fact considerably less than twelve hours, Faith acknowledged. But today, in the space of those few hours, Gianni D'Angelo had changed her whole life.

Suddenly he turned his proud head, cold, dark flashing eyes seeking out hers in a look as physical as a blow. 'I've missed out on two and a half years of my son's life. You owe me…' he murmured in sibilant condemnation.

Faith went pale and crossed her arms jerkily. 'I didn't know…I didn't remember.'

'You knew when you did your vanishing act,' Gianni reminded her darkly. 'Now go and get Connor and tell him who I am!'

Faith blinked in disconcertion. 'I can't do that—'

'Why not?' Gianni shot back at her.

'I mean, he doesn't know you…it's far too soon,' she argued.

'I won't allow you to introduce me to my own child as some passing stranger,' Gianni spelt out. 'I'm his father. At his age, he's hardly likely to be traumatised by the news!'

Put squarely on the spot, Faith studied him with strained eyes. She hadn't been prepared for that demand. Foolishly, she hadn't thought beyond letting him see Connor, and even that decision, she recognised now with sudden shame, hadn't been made for the right reasons. Playing for time, she had dangled Connor like a carrot, in an effort to soothe Gianni and prevent him from taking any other form of action.

'*Porca miseria!*' Gianni suddenly gritted in a fierce undertone, striding forward, dark eyes flaming threat. 'Does he call your fiancé Daddy?'

Faith backed off a startled step and trembled. 'No, of course not!' she gasped.

Equally as suddenly, Gianni stilled. Dark, feverish colour had sprung up over his spectacular cheekbones as he surveyed her: a slight, shivering figure with replaited hair, drawn features and frightened confused eyes. Now clad in an ugly mud-coloured jacket, flat walking shoes and a shapeless denim skirt, she looked like a waif. The bitter anger sparked by his first emotive sight of a son who didn't know him drained away. One thing hadn't changed, he acknowledged ruefully. Without him around she was still a fashion disaster, choosing comfort and practicality over style.

'It's all right, *cara*,' Gianni murmured quietly. 'Really, it's all right.'

'I don't know what I'm doing here,' Faith whispered truthfully, her vision blurring with sudden tears.

'I don't know about the location, but this meeting was definitely a step in the right direction,' Gianni told her bracingly, checking that Connor was still wholly entranced by the slide before extending a supportive arm around her. 'Take a deep breath and let it out again…'

'I might fall over…' She tried to joke, but her taut voice emerged flat as a pancake. As he eased her into the shelter of his lean body she was alarmingly conscious of his male warmth and his intimate scent. Her tummy flipped, leaving her feeling desperately ill at ease.

'Not when I'm around.'

'I really don't know why I gave you a false name,' Faith heard herself confide. 'It seems such a strange thing to have done, and I've always thought I was an honest person…I really did think that.'

Gianni tensed and suppressed a groan. The plot thickens, he conceded grimly. Of course she was going to assume that her real name was the false one. What else was she to think while she still fondly imagined that the Jenningses were her parents? But by the end of the day he would have dealt with that problem as well, he reminded himself grimly. Handling one problem at a time had become an impossible challenge.

'Take me over to Connor,' he urged.

His lack of comment surprised Faith. But then it had hardly been the right moment for that confession, she decided dully. His sole interest right now was naturally his son.

As she headed for Connor, Gianni let his arm slide from her. It felt oddly like being pushed away. Confusion assailed her. She was uneasily conscious of the change within herself. Since she had had that flashback Gianni no longer felt like a stranger. Now she was hugely aware that she had once loved him. A terrifying, all-or-nothing, no-sacrifice-too-great love, which she had apparently offered freely. But she didn't think he had ever loved her. She had sensed her own insecurity during that phone call, relived her own determined attempt to conceal that insecurity.

When he saw them coming towards him, Connor perched on the end of the slide, restlessly swinging his legs, only curiosity in his eyes as he studied Gianni. He was a friendly, confident child, who had never been shy.

'You're *big*!' he said to Gianni, his blond head falling back to take in the height of a male at least six feet three inches tall, big brown eyes wide as the sky above and openly impressed.

Gianni laughed, and immediately hunkered down to his son's level. 'I think you're going to be big too,' he commented, half to himself.

'This is…' Faith had to stop and start again as Connor gazed up at her with innocently enquiring eyes. 'This is your father, Connor.'

Connor looked blank.

'Your daddy,' Faith rephrased in a taut undertone.

He recognised that word. 'Daddy?' he repeated, small legs falling still, a puzzled look on his face. Then his dark eyes rounded and he studied Gianni with dawning wonderment. 'Peter daddy?'

As Gianni tensed, Faith crouched down beside him. 'Yes, that's right...like Peter has a daddy. This is your daddy,' she explained.

'Who's Peter?' Gianni enquired out of the corner of his mouth.

'His friend at nursery,' Faith whispered back. 'He's been to his house to play.'

'Play ball?' Connor demanded, suddenly bouncing upright in excitement. 'Daddy play ball?'

Gianni released his pent-up breath. 'Not for a long time, but willing to learn,' he muttered not quite steadily. 'Why didn't I think of bringing something like that?'

Connor danced on the spot. Peter's daddy was more of a favourite than even Faith had appreciated. 'Play cars? Phroom-phroom?' he carolled hopefully, withdrawing a tiny toy car from his pocket.

'Phroom...phroom,' Gianni sounded obediently. 'I *love* playing cars!'

Connor grinned and raised his arms to be lifted. 'Phroom...phroom...phroom!' he said exuberantly.

Gianni reached out and eased his son into his arms and then slowly came upright, a slightly stunned light in his usually keen dark eyes. He held Connor awkwardly, at a slight distance from him, visibly afraid of taking too many liberties too soon and spoiling the moment.

Reacting to the amount of attention he was receiving, Connor spread his arms and proceeded to noisily intimate an aeroplane going into freefall.

'Connor, behave!' Faith scolded in dismay, but Gianni saw his mistake and hauled his son closer before he could divebomb out of his arms.

'Daddy!' Connor exclaimed, and wound his arms round Gianni's neck to plant a big kiss on his cheek. 'My Daddy...*mine!*' he stressed, with all the satisfaction of ownership.

Faith's eyes smarted. Even at this age, her son had clearly felt the difference between himself and his friend Peter. She would never have suspected that. She had thought he was too young to appreciate the absence of a father in his life, had once assumed that the presence of her own father would fill that gap. Unfortunately, Robin Jennings worked long hours, and Connor was invariably in bed when his grandfather was at home. And Edward found the high-octane energy of a toddler difficult to handle, had frankly admitted that he would feel more at home with Connor when he was a little older.

Yet Gianni's damp eyes shone. Edward had never looked at her son with such pride and emotion and fascination. And why should he have done? Edward was not Connor's father.

'Down!' Connor demanded.

Gianni lowered him to the thick carpet of bark on the ground. Connor got cheerfully down on all fours, stuck his bottom in the air and cried, 'Woof! Woof!'

'He's doing his dog impression. You're getting his whole repertoire,' Faith explained tightly. 'He's showing off like mad.'

'He's so full of life…so sweet,' Gianni murmured huskily, hunkering down again, careless of the muddy bark welling round his superb Italian leather shoes, to stay close to his son.

Connor got bored with being a dog very quickly. 'Ducks!' he reminded his mother.

Gianni regarded Faith enquiringly.

'On the lake. He likes to see them.'

Connor had already scampered off in the direction of the lake path and Faith hurried after him. The light was fast beginning to fade. Gianni fell into step beside her. The mature trees on the woodland trail cast dark shadows. When a man suddenly stepped into view several feet ahead of them, Faith gave a start of dismay.

Gianni spoke to him in Italian, and only then did she recall the other man who had been standing above the playground.

'What's going on?' she questioned nervously as they moved on. 'Who are those men?'

'I was really surprised when I got your message earlier, particularly when you styled yourself "Milly",' Gianni admitted.

Faith coloured. 'It seemed more discreet to do that.'

'Unfortunately my security staff were convinced the message was a set-up.'

'Security staff?' Those men worked for him?

'The park is swarming with them. They've had the time of their lives staking out this place over the past hour. They love stuff like this,' Gianni conceded with wry amusement.

'Why a set-up?' she queried. 'Why would anybody think that?'

'People don't, as a rule, ask me to meet them in such public places. I did wonder if the press had finally got on to us and whether you might have received a similar message purporting to be from me. The tabloids would pay a fortune for a photo of us all together—'

'Tabloids?' she exclaimed, thoroughly taken aback.

'Wake up, *cara*. The news that I have a child will be a major scoop. And sooner or later it *will* come out,' Gianni informed her. 'I could only protect you from that exposure by staying away from my son, and I'm not prepared to do that. I won't behave as if Connor is some grubby secret in my life.'

Faith was horrified by what he was telling her. His very arrival had already exploded her quiet life out of existence. Now he was calmly admitting that there would be worse to come. Naturally the press would have an interest in the private life of a male as wealthy and powerful as Gianni. But threat of such public exposure made Faith feel ill. If it happened, her parents would be devastated, and once again she would be responsible for hurting them.

Since Connor had got down on the grass verge to play with the gravel on the path, Faith came to a halt and rested back weakly against the trunk of a tall beech tree. 'You don't give a damn, do you?' she muttered shakily. 'No matter how it affects me and my family, you'll still go ahead and demand access to Connor.'

'Guilty as charged,' Gianni said drily. 'I've been excluded from my son's life long enough.'

In the twilight, Faith focused on his lean bronzed features with a heart that was chilled even as its beat involuntarily quickened. His dark, deep-set eyes had an aggressive golden glimmer that challenged. He was tougher than titanium and he wasn't going to quit. 'You're so unfeeling,' she condemned unevenly.

Moving fluidly forward, Gianni braced one lean hand against the trunk and stared down at her, spiky black lashes low over his slumbrous gaze. 'Am I?' he questioned in a lazy undertone as smooth as black silk.

That deep, dark drawl sent tiny little shivers running down her taut spinal cord. Her bemused eyes locked to his and feverish tension snaked through her. For the space of a heartbeat she wanted to move away, and then she wasn't sure what she had wanted or even why she might have wanted it. As rational thought blurred, other more intrusive physical sensations took precedence.

That close, Gianni truly mesmerized her. Her breathing quickened, her mouth running dry. Dark excitement flowered into being inside her. Her muscles tightened on a delicious thrilling edge. The sudden aching fullness of her breasts and the urgent sensitivity of her nipples made her tremble, every pulse racing at fevered speed.

She could hardly breathe as Gianni watched her with the still golden eyes of a hunter. He brought up his other hand and let his thumb slowly graze the full curve of her lower lip. At the first touch of his hand, heat burst into being low in her pelvis, and she was betrayed into a tiny startled gasp. As Connor played at their feet, Gianni let long fingers curve to her flushed cheekbone and slowly he smiled. Faith braced herself against the tree to stay upright. That smile dazzled her, knocked her sideways, and filled her with an elemental hunger so powerful it hurt.

'Poor Edward...' Gianni husked with indolent satisfaction as he withdrew his hand and straightened again with innate grace. 'This is all about to blow up in his face. Let him go before it gets dirty, *cara*.'

Only slowly emerging from what felt vaguely like a partial black-out, Faith stared with darkened eyes up at the tall, dark male towering over her as if he had suddenly become the devil incarnate. Now she recognised the studied insolence of that smile. The frantic heat that had filled her with such mindless yearning seconds earlier now engulfed her in shame. How could she be attracted to him like this? How *could* she be? Maybe it was the disorientating sense of having one foot lodge in the past and the other foot threatening to buckle in the present. All of a sudden it was so difficult to know what she was really feeling.

'Leave Edward out of this!' she told him, with all the fierceness of her own guilty mortification.

'But he's right in the middle,' Gianni responded with supreme cool. 'So why drag out his demise? There's no contest, is there?'

'I don't know wh-what you're talking about,' Faith stammered, although she was dreadfully afraid that she did, and what he was now suggesting terrified her.

Gianni dealt her a long, slow, sardonic look. 'I don't have much compassion to spare in Benson's direction, but I'm fair enough to concede that he didn't know he was poaching on my territory...so let him go now.'

'Your territory?' Faith parroted, scarcely believing her ears.

Gianni ran a mocking fingertip down the exposed line of her extended throat and watched her jerk and instinctively lean closer. 'You're still mine, *cara*. You don't have any resistance to me at all. But then you never did have... I want you back, Milly.'

'You couldn't possibly! You're nothing to do with me any more. Our only connection now is Connor!' Faith asserted in a feverish rush of protest. Hurrying forward, she stooped to grab her son's hand and turn back the way they had come. 'It's getting dark…it's time I went home.'

'Ducks?' Connor cried in plaintive surprise.

'The ducks have gone to bed,' Faith told him with desperate urgency.

And the last sound she heard was Gianni's husky appreciative laughter.

CHAPTER FOUR

AFTER buckling a squirming complaining Connor into his car seat, Faith ruefully acknowledged that she had done it again. She had reached saturation point and fled when she could take no more. Once more Gianni D'Angelo had breached the boundaries of her expectations and forced her into uncharted waters.

His territory. She recalled that assertion with a shiver. *Gianni wanted her back.* And with that shattering statement of intent Gianni D'Angelo had plunged her into shock again. Just as she was struggling to regard and accept him as Connor's father, Gianni had revealed a motivation she had never dreamt might exist.

He had been so casual about it too, but in the cool fatalistic fashion of a male referring to an inevitable event. And he had totally unnerved her when he had urged her to let Edward go. Edward was the man she *loved*, the man she was to marry in a few months' time! Yet with frightening confidence Gianni had talked as though her fiancé was already on the way out of her life.

But mightn't she herself have unwittingly encouraged that attitude? Faith squirmed, steeped in shame over behaviour which had merely increased her emotional turmoil. Gianni was incredibly attractive, but he had one trait more disturbing and more dangerous than all the rest put together, and that was a high-voltage aura of pure sex.

She had never recognised that in a man before. But she had been susceptible, indeed had found it quite impossible to control her own intense awareness of him. But then, around Gianni she was steadily becoming a person she didn't know...

Edward hadn't come into her mind once while her wretched body had come alive like an insidious enemy. And then, as she sat there fighting to understand what was happening to her, Faith suddenly found an escape route from the daunting conviction that in responding in any way to Gianni she had betrayed Edward.

Why was she being so tough on herself? What a fool she was being! That flashback about that long-ago phone call had destabilised her. The instant she'd realised that she had once loved Gianni it had become a huge challenge to deal with him as a stranger. So for a few minutes her barriers had slipped. The line between the past and the present had blurred. And in the enervated state she was in, she had reacted in a way she would never normally have reacted...

Now that she knew the problem it wouldn't ever happen again, she told herself urgently. She had behaved as if she was still the woman making that phone call, hadn't she? She had behaved as if Gianni was her lover. So she wasn't *really* still attracted to Gianni. Involuntarily, she had responded to an eerie sense of familiarity.

Since Faith hadn't heard the limousine pulling into the car park, and certainly hadn't seen it, she almost leapt from her seat in fright when a hand gently rapped on the windscreen to attract her attention. Her head twisted round. She recognised Gianni's burgundy silk tie and it was like an instant shot of adrenalin.

Gianni opened the car door to subject her to a fulminating appraisal.

'What are you doing?' Faith demanded defensively.

'You're sitting in the dark in an unlocked car in a deserted park. You've got a lot on your mind. Let me run you home,' Gianni urged, his dark, deep drawl sending an odd little shiver through her.

'If I've got a lot on my mind, whose fault is it?' she condemned tautly. 'Why can't you give me five minutes of peace?'

'You shouldn't be on your own here.' Delivering that assurance with the supreme confidence of a male making an unarguable statement, Gianni lowered his arrogant dark head to glance into the back of the car. His brilliant dark eyes connected with hers again. 'Connor looks pretty miserable too.'

'Daddy!' Connor squealed in sudden excitement.

Flinching from that cry of recognition, Faith bowed her forehead down against the steering wheel and fought off an urge to bang it hard. But she had seen the reproof in his gaze. He hadn't needed to say anything. 'Go away, Gianni...'

'Only if you go straight home and go to bed. You're exhausted.

Faith tensed even more. She didn't *want* to go home. No longer did she feel up to dealing with her parents, who were likely to be very upset by the news that Connor's father had surfaced. Her past had caught up with her with a vengeance, and nobody was going to escape the fall-out, she acknowledged guiltily.

Lifting her head again, Faith turned the ignition key. 'I'll phone you tomorrow. I'm taking Connor to a fast-food restaurant for tea,' she announced defiantly, and, reaching out, she slammed the door loudly on Gianni.

Connor sobbed when she drove off, which really bothered her. Had he already taken that much of a liking to Gianni? Half a mile down the road, she stopped at a callbox to ring home and yet again excuse herself from a family meal. The phone rang a long time before it was answered by her father.

After she'd explained why she wouldn't be home, her father said in a curiously quiet voice. 'That's fine. Actually, we're dining out ourselves, and we'll probably be late back, so don't wait up for us. By the way, Edward's home.'

'He is?' Faith exclaimed in surprise.

'He caught an earlier flight and called in at the plant just as I was leaving,' Robin Jennings told her.

Faith drove to the restaurant. Connor ate with gusto. Faith nibbled at the odd chip and surveyed her son with her anguished heart in her eyes. Gianni had rights she couldn't deny. Gianni had had a tough deal. At lot of men who fathered children outside marriage sought to evade their responsibilities, but her son had a father who had spent three years trying to track him down. A father who showed every sign of wanting to be very much a part of Connor's life. But a father whose very existence was likely to cause Connor's mother endless hassle and grief.

Edward was home, so she knew where she was heading next. More than anybody else, her fiancé deserved to hear her news first. Edward was always calm, she reminded herself. He certainly wouldn't be happy, but surely he would ultimately take this unexpected development in his stride?

Beginning to feel like a traveller who had no place to lay her head, Faith wearily parked outside the Edwardian villa where Edward still lived with his mother. She thanked heaven that it was one of Mrs Benson's bridge nights. Connor was half asleep, and she carried him up the steps feeling like the worst of mothers for keeping him out beyond his bedtime.

Edward opened the front door and studied her in surprise. 'Faith?'

Faith chewed at her lower lip. 'Dad told me you'd got back early and I needed to see you…so here I am.'

'But why didn't you leave Connor at home?' Edward enquired.

'Mum and Dad are dining out.'

'Are you sure of that? Your father's with your mother? When I walked into Robin's office this afternoon, he was cancelling the business dinner he had arranged for tonight.' Her fiancé continued with pronounced disapproval, 'And, believe me, Bill Smith is too valuable a customer to cancel at such short notice!'

Engaged in settling Connor's limp little body into a corner of the sofa in the chilly lounge, Faith made no response. She was too worked up about what she had to tell Edward.

'Something rather unexpected has happened,' she said stiltedly.

'Everybody does seem to be acting in a very unexpected way today. Your father's evasive manner with me was distinctly odd,' Edward informed her flatly, his pale blue eyes reflecting his annoyance at what he had clearly taken as a snub.

'Look, this is *really* important, Edward,' Faith stressed.

Edward planted himself by the fireplace, a rather irritating air of indulgence in his scrutiny. 'What's up? Wedding stationery not up to scratch?'

'Something I never, ever thought was likely to happen. Connor's father, Gianni D'Angelo, has turned up!' Faith shared in a driven rush.

Edward stiffened. She certainly had his attention now. He began shooting questions at her as if she was in the witness box, charged with some kind of crime.

'Gianni D'Angelo…' Edward repeated incredulously. 'Let me get this straight. You are telling me that the electronics tycoon Gianni D'Angelo is Connor's *father*?'

'Yes, I was pretty shocked too,' Faith admitted heavily.

'Stop talking as if when all this took place it happened to somebody else!' Edward suddenly snapped accusingly. 'Believe me, I'm not too happy with the sound of all this. It's hardly what I expected, is it? Gianni D'Angelo! How on earth did you meet a man like that?'

'I don't remember, Edward—'

'Did you work for him?'

'No…' Faith began pleating a fold in her shirt with tense fingers.

'I'm starting to suspect your loss of memory might be based on a very sound instinct to bury a less than presentable past,' Edward told her in a derisive undertone.

'That's a horrible thing to say. It's not like it's something I can help,' Faith whispered painfully.

'Gianni D'Angelo…so once you moved in distinctly rarefied circles,' Edward remarked snidely, and she winced. 'What sort of relationship did you have with him?'

Stress made Faith's stomach twist. Edward's anger was already greater than she had naively anticipated, and his contempt was an equally unpleasant surprise. I can't tell him the whole truth now. I *can't*, she thought in desperation.

'As your future husband, I have the right to know, and if you don't tell me I have every intention of asking him!'

'He said...he said I was his mistress,' Faith admitted in a deadened voice. She was too exhausted to withstand any more pressure.

The silence went on and on and on. Finally she raised enough courage to look up.

Edward had gone all red in the face. He was also surveying her as if she had turned into an alien before his eyes.

'I'm very ashamed of it,' she told him unevenly.

'So that's who I'm about to marry...Gianni D'Angelo's slut.' Edward labelled her with cold venom. 'Thanks for telling me.'

Pale as milk, Faith got up and bent down to lift her son back into her arms. 'There's not much point continuing this conversation,' she replied tightly. 'You're shocked, and I understand that, but it's my past, *not* my present, Edward.'

'*Shocked* barely covers it...a sleazy association of that nature!' Edward fired back in furious disgust. 'If this gets out locally, I'll be a laughing stock!'

'Gianni's not likely to go around telling people. I only told you because it's not something I felt I could keep to myself.' Only now, she acknowledged, she very much wished she had.

Edward vented a humourless laugh. 'My mother once said I didn't know what I might be taking on with you. Clearly I should have listened!'

'Do you want your ring back?' Faith heard herself ask, without any expression at all.

Edward went rigid, bitter resentment showing in his eyes.

'Of course I don't! My God, can't I let off a little steam without you asking me that?'

'Calling me a slut is more than "a little steam",' Faith countered jaggedly, already wondering if, after their marriage, Edward would throw her past in her teeth every time she annoyed or disappointed him. 'You might as well know the lot. I was Gianni's mistress for two years…and I loved him.'

Edward surveyed her in near disbelief. Whether Faith realised it or not there had been a decided edge of defiance in that final announcement.

'Faith—' he began brusquely.

'I just want to go home, Edward. Could you open the door, please?' she asked woodenly.

Connor restored to his car seat, Faith drove off. Edward was never likely to see her in the same light again. Could she blame him for that? Edward was always very conscious of what others might think. A lot of people had seemed surprised that he should ask a single mother to be his wife. Now Edward was questioning that decision. Were his feelings for her strong enough to withstand such damaging revelations?

Arriving home to find all lights blazing, Faith carried her son straight upstairs and quickly put him to bed. Only when she went downstairs again did it occur to her that the house had the strangest air of being like the *Marie Celeste*. The kitchen even showed every sign of her mother's initial preparations for an evening meal. Faith began to tidy up, amazed that the older woman had gone out leaving potatoes half-unpeeled and the radio still playing.

Where had her parents gone in such a hurry? Her father had cancelled a business dinner and her mother should have been attending the choral evening in the church hall. It wasn't their anniversary or either of their birthdays. Their behaviour didn't make sense, but Faith was already so tired that she fell into bed, determined to suppress every anxiety and every thought.

Once she had caught up on her sleep nothing would look so bad, she assured herself. Edward would have had time to come to terms with her bombshell. He had hurt her, but possibly she had expected too much from him. After all, she too had been upset by what she had learnt about her own past today. Let the dust settle, she urged herself wearily. Tomorrow would be a whole new day.

Accustomed to being rudely awakened by Connor bouncing on her bed, Faith woke the next morning to a curious silence. Glancing drowsily at her alarm clock, she stiffened and then leapt out of bed in dismay. It was just after ten! For goodness' sake, why hadn't her mother roused her?

On her way into the bathroom Faith registered that her son's bed was already neatly made. After washing at speed, she pulled on a brown skirt and a burgundy sweater. This morning it had been her turn to open the shop early for the deliveries. A perplexed frown on her face, she hurried downstairs.

She stilled at the sight of her parents sitting together in silence in the lounge. They looked odd: stiff and strained, and somehow aged.

Robin Jennings rose heavily upright, a stocky well-built man with grey hair. 'We thought we should let you sleep in, so I called Louise first thing and said that you weren't well,' he explained. 'Then I took Connor to the nursery as usual. We need to have a serious talk with you and we felt—well, Mr D'Angelo felt it would be wiser to keep the child away from all this.'

'Mr...? Gianni...?' Faith echoed in growing confusion. 'How...I mean...oh, so you *know* about Gianni?' she suddenly gasped.

'Please sit down,' her father urged.

A hectic flush on her cheeks, Faith was instantly convinced that she knew what was happening. At that moment she absolutely loathed Gianni D'Angelo. Obviously he had gone over her head and contacted her parents. That was probably where they had been last night. *With him.* And her poor parents looked very much as if they had been completely crushed by what they had learnt about her.

'Gianni had no right to interfere!' she exclaimed furiously.

Her father grimaced. 'Faith, Mr D'Angelo—'

A slight movement at the edge of her vision made Faith spin round. She stared, dumbstruck. Gianni now stood in the archway between the lounge and the dining room. She shook her head in urgent negative. Bewildered anger and resentment burned in her questioning gaze. 'What are *you* doing here? How dare you interfere like this? How dare you go behind my back and talk to my parents?'

'That's enough, Faith,' Robin Jennings said stiffly.

'Why did you let him into this house?' Faith demanded fiercely.

Gianni strolled forward with measured steps. 'Keep quiet and sit down,' he told her, his stunning dark features stamped with gravity, his eyes impenetrable. 'I asked to be present. Robin and Davina have a rather disturbing confession to make and they need you to listen to them.'

A confession? A confession about what? Complete confusion made Faith sink slowly down into an armchair. Her accusing stare stayed on Gianni. He dominated the low-ceilinged room, with his height and presence, as alien against the backdrop of the cosy décor as a tiger prowling a busy city street. He didn't belong here, she thought bitterly, and she couldn't credit that her parents could have been influenced by any request of his.

He wore a silver-grey suit, fabulously well cut to his lithe, lean and powerful frame. The fabric had the smooth gleam of wildly expensive cloth, his shirt the sheen of silk. She clashed with dark, deep-set eyes, and suddenly it was an effort to summon up a single connected thought.

'Faith...' her father breathed curtly.

Faith looked back to her parents with some embarrassment. 'What's going on?'

'When we identified you at the hospital three years ago,

we didn't have the smallest doubt that you were our child,' the older man told her flatly. 'You were wearing the bracelet we gave our daughter on her sixteenth birthday. You were blonde, blue-eyed, about an inch taller than you had been when you left. You were a lot thinner, but then why not? Seven years is a long time.'

'Why are you talking about this?' Faith frowned.

Her mother crammed a tissue to her lips and twisted her head away with a stifled gasp. 'I can't bear this—'

'What Robin is trying to tell you is that he and his wife made a very unfortunate mistake.' Gianni advanced, sounding every word with precision.

'We were so overjoyed at getting you back,' Davina Jennings confided jerkily. 'It was over a year before I even admitted to myself that there might be room for doubt about your identity...'

Faith was now as still as a statue, her shaken eyes the only life in her taut face. 'I don't understand what you're trying to say...'

'At the start you were very ill. Then you came round and you had no memories,' Robin Jennings reminded her tensely. 'Our daughter had no distinguishing marks that we could go on. Nothing jarred at that stage. You had grown up. Naturally you had to have matured and changed.'

Gianni shot Faith's perplexed expression a perceptive glance and murmured levelly, 'They're trying to tell you that they are *not* your parents.'

'Not my parents,' Faith repeated like an obedient child. She couldn't believe that, she just couldn't believe it, couldn't even take such a gigantic concept on board long enough to consider it. 'This is crazy...why are you telling me this stuff?'

'We came to love you very much,' her father—who, according to Gianni, was *not* her father—explained almost eagerly. 'In fact as we got to know the person we believed you had become we couldn't have been happier.'

'But eventually we began making discoveries about you

that we couldn't just ignore or explain away,' Davina continued reluctantly. 'You have a lovely singing voice. Our daughter couldn't even sing in tune. You speak French like a native…our daughter failed French at GCSE. She was hopeless at languages.'

Locked suddenly into a world of her own, Faith remembered the evening her father had brought a French client home for dinner. The instant the man had uttered a French phrase she had turned without hesitation to address him in the same language. Dimly she recalled how astonished her parents had been. But at the time she hadn't thought anything of that. In fact she'd been delighted when the Frenchman had told her that she had a remarkable idiomatic grasp of his language. In those days it had seemed to her that she had no useful talents, and it had felt good to discover she had at least one.

'All the little discrepancies we'd so easily explained away at the beginning came back to haunt us. Your handwriting is so different.' Robin Jennings sighed. 'You like cats. Faith was allergic to cats. It wasn't really very likely that you'd grown out of that. We began to look rather desperately for you to remind us in some way of the daughter we remembered, but there was nothing.'

Faith sat there in the kind of shock that felt like a great weight squeezing the life force from her. 'But the bracelet…I was wearing Granny's bracelet—'

'Our daughter must've sold it. Although she took it with her when she went, she wasn't that fond of it. Perhaps you bought the bracelet, or somebody else gave it to you. We were foolish to rely so much on a piece of jewellery,' Davina conceded curtly.

'This isn't possible,' Faith said very carefully, but as the bracelet that she had long regarded as a kind of talisman was dismissed her voice sank to a mere thread of its usual volume.

Gianni released his breath in a charged hiss.

'If she doesn't want to believe it, I'm quite content,'

Davina Jennings announced, shooting a glance of bitter dislike at Gianni. 'In every way that matters she is our daughter and we love her and we don't want to lose her. Neither Robin nor I want anything to change. We told you that last night—'

'And I asked you what you intended to do if the *real* Faith showed up,' Gianni reminded the older woman without hesitation.

Davina stiffened defensively. 'Not very likely after ten years.'

'This is really happening,' Faith registered finally. 'You're telling me that I'm not really your child, that I was never your child...that this life I'm living actually belongs to another woman.'

'Your name is Milly Henner and you're twenty-four years old,' Gianni delivered. 'And while I'm here there is nothing to be afraid of.'

Milly, she thought numbly. My name *is* Milly. She fought to concentrate on thoughts that were whirling like tangled spaghetti inside her blitzed brain. She studied the people whom she had believed were her parents with a deep sense of pain and dislocation. 'How long have you known that I wasn't your daughter?'

The silence thundered. Seemingly neither wished to discuss that point.

Gianni had no such inhibition. 'They've known for about eighteen months. They only admitted their suspicions to each other then—'

'We sat up all night talking,' Robin Jennings cut in heavily. 'We just didn't know what to do. You'd accepted us. We loved you and Connor. We'd introduced you everywhere as our daughter—'

'You kept quiet sooner than face the embarrassment of admitting that you could make such an appalling mistake,' Milly, who still so desperately wanted to be Faith, condemned, at that instant hating everybody in the room. They all knew who they were and where they belonged. But she was an outsider.

'We were happy with the way things were,' Davina argued vehemently. 'Nor do we see why anything should change!'

Milly surveyed her dully.

'I will make every possible effort to trace your real daughter,' Gianni promised the older couple. 'But Milly can't stay here any longer.'

'She can if she wants to,' Robin Jennings asserted curtly.

'She can stay in touch with you. She can even visit. But as who she really is, *not* as who you'd like her to be!' Gianni's attention was on Milly's stark white face and the blank horror growing in her eyes. 'She had another life, and she needs to see that life before she makes any decisions.'

'For heaven's sake, she's engaged...she's getting married!' Davina exclaimed.

'And how do you think Edward is likely to react to this fiasco?' her husband groaned. 'I'll deal with that. I'll see him this morning and explain everything.'

With a sense of numb disbelief, Milly studied them all. Gianni stood apart, his self-discipline absolute. His dark, deep flashing eyes held hers, and she saw the pity he couldn't hide and just wanted to die. She stood up, and walked out of the room.

As Davina leapt up to follow her Gianni planted a staying hand on her arm. 'You can't help Milly with this, Mrs Jennings. Not right now, you can't,' he asserted. 'She feels betrayed by the two people she relied on most. She needs time to come to terms with this.'

'And what exactly are your plans for her, Mr D'Angelo?' the older woman demanded bitterly.

Gianni viewed his companions with concealed hostility. They might love Milly, but they had damaged her. Three years ago they had denied her the further professional help she'd needed. They had done nothing to help her regain her memory. And, unforgivably, when they had realized their mistake they had selfishly refused to put it right. They had ignored the reality that the unknown woman they had erroneously identified as their daughter must have had a life elsewhere.

They also acted as if they owned Milly, and as if she couldn't speak or think for herself. It was an attitude which filled Gianni with violent antipathy. After all, if Milly belonged to anybody, she belonged to him!

She was the mother of his son. He knew her better than anybody alive. He could put her back into the world she had left behind. Leaving Milly anywhere within reach of the Jennings would hamper her recovery. They didn't want to let go even briefly. They wanted her to go on living a fake life while he could not wait to free her from an existence that struck him as suffocating. Milly was very much a free spirit...

The free spirit stared at herself in the bedroom mirror.

Who am I? Who is Milly Henner?

This was not her home. This was not where she had grown up. Those people downstairs were not her parents. Nothing that she had believed was hers was really hers. Not the share of the shop her supposed father had insisted on buying for her, not her car, which had been a birthday present—presented on a day that probably wasn't really her birthday. Only Connor was *really* hers...

As the world she had innocently believed and trusted in caved in around her, Milly experienced an instant of pure terror that threatened to wipe her out entirely.

'Milly...come back to the hotel with me.'

She spun round and focused on Gianni. Naked loathing rippled through her. *He* had done this to her. *He* had ripped her life apart. 'I hate you...' she framed, trembling with the force of her emotions.

'You'll get over that,' Gianni informed her, without an ounce of uncertainty.

'I want Edward,' she admitted shakily, and turned away again.

'You'll get over that too,' Gianni asserted harshly.

'You can't take *him* away from me!' Milly suddenly slung wildly. 'You can take everything else but not Edward!'

'You can't love him.' Gianni's gaze was black as a stormy night, his tone pure derision. 'You can't. He's nobody; he's nothing!'

Milly's teeth gritted. 'He's the man I love!'

Gianni breathed in deep, his eyes flashing gold with raw menace. 'You couldn't possibly love a calculating little creep like that!'

'Edward is none of your business! Haven't you done enough damage?'

Gianni studied her with shimmering eyes, and then he reached for her without any warning at all. He pulled her into his powerful arms and brought his mouth down on hers. Suddenly she was on fire, her breath rasping in her throat, her slim body burning at every point of contact with his. The heated onslaught of that wide, sensual mouth was a revelation. Nothing had ever felt so necessary. Hunger clawed up through her with such greedy force that her head spun, her senses reeled. Riven with wild excitement, she pressed herself into his hard male frame with a shaken moan of surrender.

'Faith!' Davina intervened, shrill with condemnation.

As Gianni held Milly back from him she trembled in a daze of shock. She focused in startled embarrassment on the older woman lodged in the bedroom doorway.

'I'm not Faith,' she heard herself say unevenly, for she could hardly get air back into her lungs. 'I'm Milly.'

'You're still an engaged woman!' Davina turned to address Gianni. 'She's upset and confused. Why can't you leave her alone?'

Momentarily, Milly was in a world of her own. She could not credit the terrifying intensity of what Gianni had made her feel. She had behaved like a wanton, pushing closer to him and clinging. If she was mortified now, she deserved to be. But then, as the older woman had pointed out, she was upset and in no state to know what she was really feeling...

'I think it's time you told Milly the truth about her engagement,' Gianni murmured silkily.

'I haven't a clue what you're trying to imply,' Davina said thinly.

Gianni gazed down at Milly. His expressive mouth twisted. 'On your wedding day, Edward becomes a fully-fledged partner in the family firm.'

Stunned by that statement, Milly stared back at him. 'That's not true-'

'That news was to have been our wedding present to both you and Edward.' Davina tilted her chin, defying further comment.

Gianni loosed a sardonic laugh. 'Why don't you tell her the truth, Mrs Jennings? Benson got that promise before he even *asked* her to marry him!'

'That's a lie!' Milly's hands curled into tight fists by her sides as she gazed expectantly at the older woman, willing her to shoot Gianni's humiliating aspersions down in flames.

Coins of colour now embellished Davina's cheeks. 'It was a simple business agreement, Mr D'Angelo. Edward is my husband's natural successor.'

'Free partnerships are not the norm in the business world, Mrs Jennings. And you should've warned Benson to keep the news from his mother. She's ensured that half the town knows why her son is prepared to take on another man's child. You made it well worth his while,' Gianni countered very drily.

Tell me it wasn't like that, Milly wanted to beg the older woman strickenly, but she bit back the plea and straightened her shoulders to walk to the door. Only Edward could tell her what it had been like. Only Edward could convince her that he hadn't needed the bribe of a partnership in the firm to persuade him to propose.

'Where on earth are you going?' Davina demanded.

'To see Edward,' Milly looked at Gianni D'Angelo, and, try as she could, she could not suppress the sheer loathing raging through her. 'You are a complete and utter bastard!' she raked at him, heedless of the other woman's shocked gasp. 'And I don't need a memory to tell me why I left you!'

CHAPTER FIVE

REFUSING to be turned from her purpose, Milly snatched her car keys from the hall table and drove over to Jennings Engineering. On the way, she thought back over the months since she had started seeing Edward.

Right from the start he had been attentive and caring. The *dream* boyfriend for an unwed mother? a more cynical voice enquired. Certainly her pseudo-parents had heavily encouraged the relationship, but why not? As a family friend and a trusted employee, Edward had naturally impressed them as being ideal.

But Milly had been more impressed by Edward's apparent indifference to her amnesia. She had relaxed in his company. Other men she had dated had assumed that she was promiscuous just because she already had a child; Edward's respectful attitude had come as a very welcome relief. It was hardly surprising that she had fallen in love with him.

So what if it was a different kind of love from that which she had once felt for Gianni D'Angelo? From what she recalled of those emotions she imagined a lowering form of enslavement, made all the more dangerous and destructive by the strength of her sexual craving for him. There, it was out at last, she acknowledged angrily. An admission of the physical weakness which had probably got her involved with Gianni in the first place.

Yet sex barely figured in her relationship with Edward. But then what she felt for Edward was a more mature and lasting love. So cymbals didn't clash and fireworks didn't go off when Edward kissed her. But where had the cymbals and the fireworks got her before? Down and out and pregnant by a male so frighteningly ruthless she could only admire herself for walking out on him three years earlier.

Milly parked the car outside the small office block beside the engineering plant. She was relieved that Robin Jennings was still at home. She had had enough of other people's interference.

A nightmare mistake had been made, but she was OK, she told herself bracingly; she was coping. Gianni had tried to destroy everything, but as long as she still had Edward she would manage to come to terms with all the rest. She blocked out the little voice that warned that she was hanging by her fingernails onto her last shred of control.

Edward was in his office. Her unannounced entrance made him rise from behind his desk in surprise. Strain from their contentious meeting the night before showed in the stiffness of his greeting.

'I was going to call you this afternoon,' he told her rather defensively.

'I needed to see you to talk. This morning I found out something that I wish you'd thought to share openly with me,' Milly admitted tautly.

'Unlike your life, mine is an open book,' Edward retorted crisply. 'I've kept nothing from you.'

'What about the partnership you get the day you marry me?' Milly enquired, wanting him to tell her that that was a very twisted version of the truth.

Edward stiffened. 'Your parents told me they wanted that news to be a surprise. Naturally I didn't discuss it with you.'

Her knees now unreliable supports, Milly dropped down on the arm of a chair. 'Would you have asked me to marry you without that partnership, Edward?' she asked tightly. 'Please be honest.'

Edward's fair complexion reddened. 'That is a very unfair question.'

'But you're not denying that the partnership was put on the table *before* you decided to propose, are you?'

Edward studied her with unconcealed resentment. 'I don't

see why you should have a problem with that. Your father's generous offer meant that we could have a financially secure future together. Of course it made a difference.'

Nausea pooled in Milly's stomach. 'What about love?'

'I'm very fond of you. But I'd be a liar if I didn't admit that I was also very concerned about the risks of forming a lasting relationship with you.'

'Risks?'

'Do I have to spell it out? That bombshell you dropped on me last night wouldn't have occurred in a *normal* relationship!' he reminded her with derision. 'Like any other man, I want to feel confident that I know everything there is to know about my wife's past. You can't give me that confidence.'

'But the assurance of a financially secure future persuaded you to overlook those drawbacks,' Milly gathered, struggling to keep her voice level. 'Yet you *said* you loved me.'

'For pity's sake, you're talking like a silly teenager-'

'I think maybe I still am just a teenager inside, Edward. If I had had any idea how many reservations you had about me, I'd never have agreed to marry you.' Tugging the solitaire from her finger, Milly stood up to place it on the edge of his desk.

Edward was outraged. 'You *asked* me to be honest!'

But he had been cruelly belittling her from the minute she started speaking, Milly reflected painfully. 'When you hear what your boss has to tell you, I think you'll be relieved to have that ring back. I imagine he'll offer you the partnership anyway. I do wish you well, Edward.'

Striding forward, he snapped bruising fingers round her slender wrist to prevent her departure. 'Who do you think you are to talk to me like this?' he demanded contemptuously.

Milly was shaken. 'Let go of me…you're hurting me—'

'I found your attitude equally offensive last night,' Edward snapped furiously. 'It seems to me that the minute you discovered that Connor's father was a rich man, you got

too big for your boots! Now put that ring back on and we'll
say no more about this nonsense!'

Taken aback as she was by his aggression, Milly was
relieved when a knock sounded on the door and his secretary
interrupted them. Edward released her immediately. Milly
hurried down the corridor, ignoring his call in his wake. And
then, out at Reception, she hesitated and looked at the car
keys still clutched in her hand. She left them with the receptionist for Robin Jennings to collect. Suddenly she
wanted *nothing* that had belonged to Faith Jennings...

Edward had never loved her. Indeed, right from the start
Edward had had serious reservations about a woman with a
past she couldn't remember. Without the partnership deal he
would never have proposed. And why had she never noticed
what a bad-tempered bully Edward could be if he was
crossed? The answer was that until last night she had never
crossed or challenged Edward. She had been a doormat,
ashamed of her unwed mother status, thinking herself very
fortunate to be the intended wife of a respectable professional man. And who had given her such low expectations
and such a poor self-image? Her fake parents, who had pack-
aged her up with a lucrative partnership to persuade Edward
to marry her.

There was a stiff breeze blowing and it was cold. Milly
had left her jacket locked in the car, but she still hurried
away from the engineering plant. When she found herself
on the main road she just kept on walking, insensibly
soothed by the noise of the anonymous traffic. All the shocks
she had withstood over the past twenty-four hours were hitting her now full force. Edward had seemed like a safe and
sturdy post to clutch in the storm, but the post had toppled
when she had reached for its support. The oddest thing was
that she couldn't yet feel a single shard of grief. But then,
she acknowledged dully, she wasn't really feeling anything...

'*Where the hell is she?*' Gianni raked into the phone.

'We've found her. She's OK. She's sitting on a bench by

the lake in that park.'

'*Madre di Dio!*' Gianni launched, paling at that information. 'I want two of you within six feet of her until I get there!'

After telling his driver to go as fast as the speed limit would allow, Gianni threw back a brandy to steady himself. He was furious with himself. He had known he had to go slowly with Milly. The psychologist had warned him to be careful. But from the first moment he had wildly overplayed his hand.

He should have kept quiet about Benson and the partnership. He had planned to hold that in reserve for a few days. Yet he, who had the reputation for being a brilliant tactician with a superb sense of timing, had ploughed in like a bull in a china shop. The prospect of reaping his own just deserts didn't bother him. But he went into a cold sweat at the threat of Milly reaping them for him...

Milly knew she was being watched at the lake. The instant she recognised the dark-suited men trying not to draw attention to themselves and failing abysmally in their efforts to lurk behind winter-bare trees she almost smiled. Gianni's employees. He must have had her followed. As long as they left her alone, it was almost comforting to think that somebody was looking out for her.

That sound of brisk footsteps made her lift her head. Gianni was bearing down on her, his hard, bronzed features set in grim lines which detracted not one iota from his devastating good looks, she conceded absently. A light grey cashmere overcoat protected him from the chilly breeze ruffling his luxuriant black hair.

'This is a very dreary place.' Both disapproval and impatience rang from every syllable. Gianni slung a deeply unappreciative glance over his surroundings. '*And* it's freezing. Why haven't you got a coat on?'

Even before he peeled off his overcoat and dropped it round her with the pronounced casualness of a male who didn't want to make a production out of doing it, Milly's sense of isolation lessened. Gianni was exasperated and he was letting her see the fact.

'What the hell are you smiling at?' Gianni demanded, thrown by that slight undeniable tilt to her formerly tense mouth.

Almost drowning in the heavy, enveloping folds of his overcoat, and curiously soothed by the warm scent of him that still clung to the silk-lined garment, Milly gazed up at him with rueful blue eyes. 'I don't know.'

'Why did you leave your car behind at the engineering plant? Did it break down?'

'It's not my car. The Jenningses bought it when they still thought I was their daughter. I guess I'm not in a very practical mood,' Milly conceded.

As she lifted her hand to prevent his overcoat lurching off her shoulder, Gianni muttered something raw in his own language and caught her fingers in his. Milly stiffened as he scrutinised the blue-black bruising encircling her wrist.

'You damned well didn't do that to yourself!' Gianni bit out wrathfully.

Milly tugged her hand free and hurriedly curved it out of sight again.

'*Per meraviglia!* The cowardly little bastard,' he growled, well-nigh incredulous, it seemed, that anybody should have dared to lay a rough hand on her. 'I'll make him pay for hurting you!'

'No, you won't,' Milly whispered flatly. 'Those bruises came cheap at the price of what they taught me. Maybe I'm wronging Edward, but I suspect he would have lashed out in temper again once we were married. He really did feel that he was marrying beneath himself. He could never have accepted me as I am.'

Gianni glanced at her other hand, only now noticing the absence of the diamond engagement ring. Milly watched his eloquent dark eyes shimmer with unadulterated satisfaction. On the most basic level, she was beginning to understand

Gianni. He was delighted that her engagement was broken. He wouldn't waste his breath uttering empty conventional regrets.

'I don't have *any* close relatives, do I?' Milly prompted abruptly.

Gianni frowned.

That frown was answer enough for Milly. She averted her head, determined not to betray that a foolish glimmer of hope had just been extinguished.

'How did you work that out for yourself?' It was the tone of a very clever male unaccustomed to being second-guessed.

'If I'd had a genuine suffering close relation waiting somewhere for word of me, you'd have been sure to tell Robin and Davina so that they could feel even worse.'

A laugh of reluctant appreciation was torn from Gianni.

'So, since everybody starts out with parents,' Milly continued doggedly, 'I presume mine are long gone.'

'Your mother when you were eight, your father shortly before we met,' Gianni confirmed unemotionally. 'You were an only child. As far as I'm aware there were no other relatives.'

So, but for Connor, she really was alone.

'Let's go,' Gianni reached down, closed his hand firmly over hers and tugged her upright to walk her back along the path. 'Why did you come here anyway?'

'I've spent a lot of happy times here with Connor...but today I felt lost,' she admitted reluctantly.

'Even the worst situations have at least one positive aspect. You've had an extraordinary experience,' Gianni told her. 'How many people get the chance to live more than one life?'

Disconcerted, Milly blinked. That reality hadn't crossed her mind once.

'Right now you're between lives, but no way are you lost. You've got me,' Gianni delivered with supreme cool.

'You make it all sound so simple.'

'It is. You don't belong here. That's why you feel strange. I know you care about the Jenningses, but they didn't do you any favours. If they hadn't claimed you, I'd have found you ages ago,' Gianni reminded her grimly.

'Did you list me as missing?'

'Of course I did!' Gianni growled, as if he was insulted by the idea that she could think otherwise.

'I *so* wish you'd found me first…' That thought had translated itself into charged admission before she could think better of it. She tensed. All the barriers she had tried to put up against Gianni had somehow tumbled down. It made her feel very vulnerable.

'Luck wasn't on my side. You walked out of the apartment of your own free will. There were no suspicious circumstances, so the police weren't interested. Adults have the right to lose themselves if they want to,' Gianni informed her wryly.

As they reached the park exit the limousine drew up, and Milly climbed in without protest.

Only a couple of hours ago she had hated Gianni D'Angelo like poison. He had been the destroyer. He had been the target of all her furious disbelief and bitter resentment. But now, as he used the car phone and talked in fluid Italian, she studied him with helpless intensity. The strong bone structure, the straight, arrogant nose, the firmly chiselled mouth. The dangerous dark eyes that knew too much, saw too much, and which he could turn on her like a weapon to express more than most people could say in five minutes. Those eyes were spectacular in the frame of that lean, dark face.

His gaze narrowed slumbrously, his arrogant dark head tilting back almost as if he was inviting her appraisal to continue. The elegant, sexily indolent sprawl of his long, lean, powerful body made her breath shorten in her throat, her heart thump against her breastbone. He really was *so* beautiful…

Colour ran up beneath her complexion and she tore her

attention from him, dismay and embarrassment darting through her. How could she be thinking such thoughts now? And she could feel herself wanting to trust him, but how could she trust him when she couldn't even trust herself? If she had learned anything over the past hours, it was that every single thing came at a price.

'Did you say you wanted me back because of Connor?' She got even redder as she spoke, knowing that she was being too blunt.

'No,' Gianni drawled, with all the cool she lacked. 'I wouldn't pretend even for the sake of my son. If you tried to deny me access to him, I would fight you through legal channels, but I believe you already accept that Connor has a right to get to know his father.'

'Yes.' Milly was impressed by that clear-minded reading of the situation. Succinct, realistic, fair.

On the drive through town, the limo pulled up on the main street. Gianni buzzed a window down. One of his security men passed in a large shallow box stamped with the logo of a newly opened pizza parlour. Seconds later, the limo rejoined the traffic.

Gianni settled the box on her lap without ceremony. 'You're crazy about pizza.'

'Am I?' Pizza wasn't something that featured on the menu in the Jenningses' home, and Edward despised all fast food.

'You didn't even have breakfast this morning. You need to eat something before we go and collect Connor.' Gianni poured her a soft drink from the built-in bar. 'Why are you staring at me?'

'No reason...' Possibly it was the combination of the vast, opulent limo, the humble pizza box and Gianni's total lack of snobbery. Or possibly it was the regularity with which he seemed to act to ensure her well-being. And always without comment or fanfare, as if it was the most natural thing in the world that he should take care of her.

Touched by that comforting thought, after the lack of caring Edward had demonstrated when the chips were down,

Milly opened the box. She lifted out a warm, flavoursome wedge and was surprised to feel her tastebuds water. 'Aren't you having any?'

'I'm not hungry.'

But Milly was ravenous, and nothing had ever tasted so good as that pizza. When she could eat no more, she sat unselfconsciously licking her fingers clean until some sixth sense made her lift her head. Gianni's burnished gaze roamed intently from her wet fingertip to her moist pink rounded mouth and flashed a message of very masculine hunger straight into her widening eyes. The atmosphere was electric.

Her breathing fracturing, Milly shifted on the seat. A starburst of heat blossomed between her thighs, making her flush with discomfiture. Shaken by a response that she couldn't control, she shivered. All of a sudden she was painfully conscious of the ripe fullness of her breasts and the swollen tightness of her nipples. The sexual sizzle in the air unnerved her. And Gianni's tension was patent. Feverish colour lay in a hard line over his taut cheekbones. Her pupils dilating, she stared wordlessly back at him, torn by a bewildering mixture of excitement, fear and fascination.

'I know I can't touch you. Don't tease me, ' Gianni breathed in charged reproof.

In sudden embarrassment, Milly closed her eyes to shut him out. 'I'm not like that…like *this*!' she stressed in denial.

'Stretch your imagination. Once you regarded a healthy desire to rip my clothes off as the most natural thing in the world.' His deep-pitched drawl was as abrasive as sand sliding over silk. 'It was the same for both of us. I once withstood a flight of sixteen hours just to spend two hours with you and then fly right back again.'

That deep, dark drawl scent erotic images that made her squirm skimming into her mind's eye. He had flown halfway across the world just to spend two hours with her? She was stunned by that knowledge. And was there a woman alive who wouldn't feel her self-esteem enhanced by such an extravagant gesture?

'Every time we made love felt like the first time. Endless variations on the same glorious theme. The hunger was never satisfied. I don't like anything that comes between me and control,' Gianni confessed huskily. 'But nobody else has ever made me feel the way you can make me feel. So if I'm not ashamed of it, why should you be?'

And Milly listened, *of course* she listened, drinking in every word, taken aback and then impressed by his honesty. It no longer felt quite so indecent to experience a sudden violent longing to be in his arms. Past chemistry had to be operating on her, a powerful physical sense of familiarity. And at least Gianni really genuinely wanted her, she found herself thinking helplessly. Edward hadn't, not really.

And Gianni had nothing to gain and no reason to lie to her. She respected his need to forge a relationship with his son. He already knew she wouldn't try to keep them apart. He was being so kind today. So why had he seemed so very cold and hostile to her yesterday?

Perhaps he had just felt awkward. Perhaps he had been apprehensive of her reaction to the idea of having to share her son. She had been overwrought, confused and angry. Her initial reactions to him would have been far from reassuring, she decided.

'I've booked the suite above mine for you and Connor,' Gianni divulged lazily as the limo pulled up outside Connor's nursery.

Milly glanced up and met his eyes in dismay. 'I—'

'You have to make that break. It's up to you whether you do it now or later. But if you stay with the Jenningses you're likely to find yourself being put under more pressure, and you have enough to cope with right now. They're not ready to accept that things have changed.'

Things have changed. Such a bland description of the shattering new knowledge that had virtually wiped out the past three years of her life. But to move straight out into a hotel? Gianni's hotel? She needed to stand on her own feet, no matter how difficult it was. But Gianni *was* Connor's father. Surely she could trust him that far? She badly needed a quiet corner where she could lick her wounds, pull herself together and decide what to do next.

'Would you leave me alone?'

'If that's what you want.'

She wasn't at all sure it was, but somehow it had seemed safer to give him that impression.

'But I'd like to spend time with Connor,' Gianni completed.

'I'd have gone to my friend, Louise…but she wouldn't have room for us.'

She went to collect Connor. He did an excited dance on the pavement when he saw the big car. One look at Gianni and his whole face lit up. Connor scrambled into the back seat and wedged himself cheerfully as close as he could get to Gianni.

'Phroom-phroom!' he urged with a grin, impatient for the limo to move off again.

Milly's heart clenched when she saw Gianni meet that satisfied grin with one of his own. A startlingly easy, natural smile such as he had never shown her. It wiped every scrap of reserve from his lean bronzed features and was, she sensed, a rare event. Can I trust him…dare I trust him? What have I got to lose?

Gianni watched Milly pace restively round the dimly lit and spacious reception room, her slender body rigid as a bowstring.

So far her control had been too good to be true. A return visit to the Jenningses' home had been yet another distressing experience for her. She had been greeted with recriminations about her treatment of Edward and shocked reproaches at the speed with which she was moving out. And Gianni had been as welcome as the Grim Reaper calling in at a christening.

However, Milly had still sat down with Robin and Davina

Jennings to tell them how truly grateful she was for all they had done for her. In fact, Milly had shone like a star. She had said and done all the right things. She had come across as loyal, compassionate and forgiving. It had been a hell of an impressive show. But Gianni had watched her like a hawk, waiting for a fleeting expression to reveal to his cynical eyes at least that it was all just a clever act.

Yet once Gianni had fully believed that what you saw *was* what you got with Milly. But no decent woman would have betrayed him with his own brother for the sake of a quick sexual fix. He had realised then that Milly had to have a really shallow core which she was outstandingly good at keeping hidden. Bitter anger lanced through Gianni at that knowledge. No way was he about to allow her to suck him in with that I'm-so-nice act again!

So why *was* he still hanging about, holding her hand and being supportive? She didn't deserve that sort of stuff any more. She was playing him like a little lapdog on a lead! Just because she looked all fragile and forlorn, so touchingly brave in the face of adversity! Gianni slung her a brooding appraisal and then stiffened. What a total idiot he was being! A billionaire turning up to reclaim her had to be of considerable comfort! No wonder she wasn't coming apart at the seams! Suddenly he wished he had shown up in a battered old car and pretended to be poor...

His lean, strong face grim, Gianni strode rigid-backed towards the door. 'Call Room Service when you want to eat,' he told Milly.

Milly stopped pacing, shadowed blue eyes flying to him in unconcealed dismay. 'Where are you going?'

'Look, all this stuff is taking a large chunk out of my work schedule,' Gianni informed her flatly. 'Just thought I'd mention it.'

Milly's lower lip trembled. He sounded so fed up with her, but when she thought about what he had had to put up with over the past day or so, suddenly she wasn't the least bit surprised by the way he was behaving. Her wobbly mouth made a determined stab at an apologetic smile. 'I'm really sorry, Gianni.'

Gianni shifted one broad shoulder in an infinitesimal and very Latin shrug. 'What for?'

'Because I've been really selfish,' Milly acknowledged guiltily. 'You've been dragged into the midst of all my problems and this morning I was even calling you names! If it wasn't for you, I'd still be thinking I was Faith Jennings. But not once have I stopped to say thank you—'

'I don't want gratitude.'

Milly looked uncertainly at him. Sensing his eagerness to be gone, she suppressed the awareness that she didn't want to be alone with only her own thoughts to keep her company. She wasn't a baby. She had to manage.

'Could you bring your work up here?' she nonetheless heard herself ask.

'I have half a dozen staff working flat out. I doubt if Connor would sleep through the racket.'

Milly nodded slowly, forced an understanding smile and turned away.

Gianni opened the door.

'How do I get in touch with you if I need to?' she suddenly spun back to demand.

Gianni stilled. 'I'm only one floor below you,' he pointed out drily.

'So what's the number of your suite?' she prompted anxiously.

Gianni studied her for a long, tense moment, brilliant dark eyes veiled. 'I'll send a mobile phone up...OK?'

Her throat thickening, she nodded again.

He compressed his expressive mouth even more. 'You can call me as much as you want...all right?'

Milly kept on nodding like a puppet.

She wouldn't call. He wouldn't want to be interrupted. But didn't he realise that she needed to talk? She stopped herself dead on that censorious thought. Exactly when had she begun pinning so many expectations on Gianni? Maybe right at this moment she badly needed to believe that Gianni really cared about what happened to her, but that didn't give her an excuse to cling to him.

Yet Gianni was the only person who *knew* Milly Henner, her one connection, her sole link to twenty-three years of her life. Everything she had ever told him about herself was locked inside that proud dark head of his. But he wasn't parting with any of it in a hurry, was he? He was sitting on all that information like a miser on a gold mountain!

With Gianni gone, Milly made herself order a meal. Connor was fast asleep in one of the two bedrooms. He had had tea before she'd left her former home. After the fastest bath on record, she had changed him into his pyjamas and tucked him into bed. Already overtired, he had slept within minutes.

Milly took her time eating, but tasted nothing. Then she went for a long shower, donned a pale blue cotton nightdress and carefully dried her hair. When she emerged from the bedroom, the mobile phone Gianni had sent up was buzzing like an angry wasp on the coffee table.

She picked it up. 'Yes?'

'Why the blazes haven't you called me?' Gianni demanded rawly.

'I didn't want to bother you.'

'How am I supposed to work when I'm worrying about why you haven't called?' Gianni gritted.

'I'm sorry. I didn't realise you were worrying.' Milly sank down on the nearest sofa, much of her extreme tension evaporating under that comforting assurance. 'Gianni, can I ask you some questions now about us?'

'You're limited to three.'

'How did we meet?'

'You jumped out of my birthday cake. Next question.'

'I...I did *what*?' Milly gasped, thunderstruck. 'Honestly?'

'Honestly, and only two more questions to go,' Gianni reminded her.

'Why...why did I leave you?' she asked awkwardly.

Silence thundered on the line.

'That one's on the forbidden list,' Gianni responded flatly.

'That's not fair,' Milly protested. 'I mean, obviously I want to know that!'

'I'm not telling you. When you've come up with a replacement question, call me back,' Gianni suggested drily.

The line went dead.

Had Gianni done something dreadful to make her walk out? Had she done something dreadful? Or had they had a foolish argument in which one of them or both of them had said too much? An argument which struck Gianni as so stupid in retrospect that it really galled him to even think of it now?

She waited ten minutes and then she punched out the number that had arrived with the phone.

'It's me,' she announced.

'I know it's you,' Gianni breathed wryly.

'Second question,' she began rather tautly after his last response. 'Was I happy with you?'

'I thought you were deliriously happy, but that's not really a question I can answer for you.'

In the last three years, Milly had known not one minute of what she could have termed *delirious* happiness. The concept of such an extreme couldn't help but impress her to death.

'Gianni...what was I like then?'

'Stubborn, quick-tempered, full of life, unconventional...hell, this isn't a safe subject!'

Milly snatched in a ragged breath, still reeling in astonishment from that disturbing flood of adjectives.

'Are you OK?'

A choked sob was lodged in her throat. 'Fine,' she managed. 'I think I'll go to bed now.'

Milly Henner, it seemed, had been another woman entirely. A definite individual. Lively, strong...*unconventional*? A humourless laugh escaped Milly as she climbed into bed. Gianni's description had knocked her for six.

She had judged their past relationship on the basis of the narrow outlook she had developed over the past three years. His mistress. She had been shocked, ashamed. She had immediately seen herself as a victim. But Gianni hadn't described a woman who was a victim; Gianni had described an equal. Where had that stronger and more confident woman gone? And was she ever going to find her again?

Exhaustion sent Milly to sleep quickly, but dreams full of disturbing and increasingly frightening images kept her tossing and turning. Terror began to rise notch by notch until finally she came awake in a complete panic, shaking like a leaf and sobbing out loud, so confused she didn't even know where she was.

'*Dio mio, cara*...calm down!'

The instant she heard Gianni's voice she froze, and then just crumpled into the shelter of his arms, sick with relief that he was there.

CHAPTER SIX

A SOB catching in her throat, Milly pressed her damp face into Gianni's shoulder. The faint tang of expensive cologne underlying his own distinctive male scent made her nostrils flare. She breathed him in deep, like a drug.

'That must have been some nightmare, *cara*.' Gianni held her back from him.

Her eyes were huge and shadowed in the stark white triangle of her face. 'I was struggling with someone in the dark...it felt so *real*!'

'But it couldn't have been. Nothing like that ever happened to you, at least not when I knew you.' Gianni spread long fingers across her taut cheekbones, dark, deep flashing eyes scanning her still frightened face.

Some of her tension drained away at that comforting assurance, but not all of it. She had never had a dream like that before, could not help suspecting that something she had once experienced had summoned it up.

'Before you woke up, you called my name at the top of your voice,' Gianni imparted softly, mesmeric dark eyes glinting.

'Did I?' Milly didn't want to talk about the dream any more. It had scared her too much. Her brows drew together. 'How did you hear me...I mean, where on earth did you come from?' she belatedly thought to ask.

'About thirty feet away,' Gianni told her. 'I'd moved to work in the room next door. I didn't think you should be alone tonight, so I came up about an hour ago. If you hadn't wakened, you'd never have known I was there.'

In the dim light, Milly studied him properly for the first time. Shorn of his jacket and tie, his white silk shirt open at his strong brown throat and his black hair slightly tousled, he looked infinitely more approachable than he usually did. A faint blue-black shadow had already darkened his aggressive jawline. Even stubble, she thought guiltily, added to his appeal. Hurriedly she turned her head away and made herself rest back against the pillows.

'I'll get back to work.' Gianni began to stand up.

Milly tensed in dismay. 'Do you have to?'

'You want me to stay?'

Milly nodded agreement. 'And talk about something cheerful. You could tell me about my parents, if you like.'

Gianni folded down on the bed, stretched his long, lean frame out with intrinsic grace and sent her a winging glance from beneath heavily lidded eyes. 'You know what's going to happen, don't you?' he murmured, like an indolent tiger.

'Nothing's going to happen.' Milly reddened. 'Think of the bed as a sofa.'

Gianni loosed a low-pitched laugh and tilted his arrogant dark head back against the white pillows. 'Your parents…you told me they were crazy about each other. Your father was called Leo and he was a Londoner. Your mother, Suzanne, was French—'

'French?' Milly rolled over in surprise to stare at him.

'You're practically bilingual. Didn't you find that out yet? You spent the first eight years of your life in Paris.'

'You're supposed to start at the beginning. Do you know when my parents got married?'

'They didn't…they weren't into matrimony.'

Milly was stunned. 'You mean, I'm…?'

'Yes.'

She slowly shook her head. Her throat tickled, and then the laughter just bubbled out of her.

Gianni leant down, curved his hands to her shaking shoulders and tugged her up to his level. 'What's so funny?'

Struggling to get a grip on herself again, Milly released a rueful groan. 'It's just so ironic. In the world I've been living in for the past three years illegitimacy is a very serious issue, and now I find out that *I* was born out of wedlock too! Tell me about Leo and Suzanne,' she urged.

'They were pavement artists.'

'Pavement artists,' Milly repeated weakly, and then she smiled. 'I like that.'

'Suzanne was knocked down and killed by a drunk driver in Paris. Your father never really got over it, and that was the end of your settled home life. He took you roving all over Europe with him. You didn't see the inside of too many schools, but you adored your father and you always talked as if you'd had a wonderful childhood.'

Milly gazed up into Gianni's lean bronzed face like a child listening to an enthralling bedtime story. 'I'm glad.'

'But then you always were a sunny optimist.' Gianni skimmed a lazy forefinger lightly through the glossy strands of blonde hair tumbling across his forearm and stared down at her with glittering dark golden eyes.

Her heart skipped a beat and then began to thud heavily. Her stomach clenched. The silence lingered and Gianni's eloquent mouth tipped into an indolent smile that welded her attention to him.

'I'm a real pessimist about most things,' Gianni shared softly. 'But in one field I'm rarely disappointed...'

A curious languor had crept over Milly. Her body felt weighted, yet incredibly alive, every sense feeling somehow keener, sharper. What a wonderful voice he had, she thought absently, as a little tremor ran down her taut spinal cord. Like sinfully rich chocolate. *Sin*... Her abstracted brain began to play with the word. *Sin*fully stunning, *sin*fully sexy...

Hot pink staining her cheekbones, she attempted to concentrate on what he was saying—which was a little difficult, she discovered, when he wasn't actually saying anything!

Slumbrous golden eyes framed with lush ebony lashes rested on her. And, like a tidal wave, Milly felt an enormous rush of yearning well up inside her. She remembered that sensational kiss. The cymbals...the fireworks. Unwittingly, she began to lift her head, push up on one elbow, soft lips tremulously parted, her slim length beginning to curve towards him as if he was a magnet and she was a nail.

'And you have never once disappointed me in that field,' Gianni informed her huskily.

Milly hadn't a clue what he was talking about, and couldn't have strung two rational thoughts together. 'Didn't I?' she managed breathlessly.

'In that one corner of our relationship I had total and absolute control.' Gianni's wide, sensual mouth curved into a wickedly charismatic smile that squeezed her heart in a sneak attack.

The dim light accentuated the smooth dark planes and hollows of his chiselled features. His bronzed skin was vibrant against the pristine whiteness of his shirt. With one long, lean and powerful thigh raised in a very masculine attitude of relaxation, Gianni was so physically arresting he just took her breath away.

In fact, she was so tense her muscles hurt. Yet she couldn't make herself move, couldn't drag her eyes from him, couldn't suppress the increasingly desperate craving holding her so still. Gianni bent his dark head slowly. His breath fanned her cheek. He let his tongue dart between her parted lips and she jerked and moaned and reached up for him, her hands spearing fiercely into his silky black hair.

He did it again, and her whole body leapt, electrified. Just one kiss, just one kiss, she promised herself, like an alcoholic craving what she knew she shouldn't have.

'Oh Gi-anni…' she gasped on the back of an aching sigh.

He pressed his mouth to her cheek, her brow, her lowered eyelids, teasing her with feather-light kisses until she strained up to him even more. 'Any time, any place, any way I want,' Gianni murmured thickly. 'I don't have to say anything, I don't have to do anything. I just start thinking about sex and you are so tuned in to me you just *melt*…'

He kissed her, and it was like being shot to heaven on a rocket. She melted to boiling point in seconds. He made love to her mouth with an intimacy that shook her. He delved and tasted and skimmed until she was burning up, clutching at him, living from one second to the next on the single terrifying thought that he might stop.

Peeling her hands from him, Gianni lowered her back to the bed. He sat up and ripped off his shirt in one impatient movement. Struggling to get air back into her constricted lungs, Milly was totally transfixed. He had a torso like a Greek god. Wide brown shoulders, rippling pectoral muscles roughened by a triangle of black curling hair and a stomach as flat as a washboard.

A tiny pinching sensation attacked low in her pelvis. She felt light-headed, but her body was so tense it screamed at her, every sense recognising Gianni as her lover. The scent of him, the touch of him, the very taste of him. She couldn't believe what was happening to her. She shivered in shock laced with a kind of death-defying excitement.

'Gianni…' she whispered jaggedly, struggling to reinstate some form of control, some sense of reality to her own mounting disorientation. 'I…*we*—'

Gianni came back down to her, dark eyes now bright as flames, his feverish tension as marked as her own. She saw a hunger in him that twisted something painfully inside her, and with a muffled little sound of surrender she reached up instinctively and opened her lips to him again.

With a dark, driven groan of satisfaction, Gianni lifted her up to him with two powerful hands and ravaged the tender interior of her mouth with a raw, demanding passion that overwhelmed her.

'We both need this,' he said thickly. 'You want me; you *always* want me…'

She looked at him, her heart pounding like crazy. She raised a trembling hand and touched his beautiful mouth with tender caressing fingertips, controlled by instincts that filled her with almost unbearably powerful feelings. 'Like I need air to breathe,' she whispered shakily.

Gianni raised her up and divested her of her nightdress

Dear Reader,

Because you've chosen to read one of our fine romance novels, we'd like to say "thank you!" And, as a <u>special</u> way to thank you, we've selected <u>two more</u> of the books you love so well, <u>plus</u> an exciting mystery gift, to send you absolutely **FREE!**

Please enjoy them with our compliments...

Rebecca Pearson

Editor

P.S. And because we <u>value</u> our customers, we've attached something extra inside...

EDITOR'S FREE GIFT SEAL THANK YOU

Peel off seal and Place inside...

How to validate your
Editor's FREE GIFT "Thank You"

1. Peel off gift seal from front cover. Place it in space provided at right. This automatically entitles you to receive 2 FREE BOOKS and a fabulous mystery gift.

2. Send back this card and you'll get 2 brand-new Harlequin Presents® novels. These books have a cover price of $3.99 each in the U.S. and $4.50 each in Canada, but they are yours to keep absolutely free.

3. There's no catch. You're under no obligation to buy anything. We charge nothing—ZERO—for your first shipment. And you don't have to make any minimum number of purchases—not even one!

4. The fact is, thousands of readers enjoy receiving their books by mail from the Harlequin Reader Service®. They enjoy the convenience of home delivery...they like getting the best new novels at discount prices BEFORE they're available in stores...and they love their *Heart to Heart* subscriber newsletter featuring author news, horoscopes, recipes, book reviews and much more!

5. We hope that after receiving your free books you'll want to remain a subscriber. But the choice is yours— to continue or cancel, any time at all! So why not take us up on our invitation, with no risk of any kind. You'll be glad you did!

6. Don't forget to detach your FREE BOOKMARK. And remember...just for validating your Editor's Free Gift Offer, we'll send you THREE gifts, *ABSOLUTELY FREE!*

GET A **FREE** MYSTERY GIFT...

YOURS FREE!

SURPRISE MYSTERY GIFT COULD BE YOURS _FREE_ AS A SPECIAL "THANK YOU" FROM THE EDITORS OF HARLEQUIN

Visit us online at
www.eHarlequin.com

with an easy expertise that somehow shocked her. And suddenly that wholly inborn feeling of security abandoned Milly. She stared in dismay down at the ripe swell of her bare breasts, her face hot with colour. She felt wanton, and then very, very shy as Gianni's gaze burned over her exposed flesh like the kiss of fire.

'*Dio…*' he growled, raising an unsteady hand to cup a pale, pouting breast adorned by a straining pink nipple, lingering to rub a thumb and forefinger over that stiffened peak.

The violence of her own response tore a startled moan from Milly. Her mind closed in on itself again, stripping away that brief awareness of anything beyond the physical. She shut her eyes tight, letting her head fall back. As he toyed with the achingly sensitive bud her own heartbeat thrummed in her eardrums.

'I always adored your breasts. You're exquisite,' Gianni groaned, knotting one possessive hand into her cascading mane of golden hair and letting his mouth swoop down to replace his fingers.

Excitement took hold of her like a bushfire, blazing out of her control. The erotic mastery he unleashed with the tug of his teeth and the wet rasp of his tongue dragged her down so fast into a world of pure sensation that she was lost. She moaned and twisted, suddenly hotter than she could bear. She was wildly aware now of the maddening burn at the very core of her body, the pulse of damp warmth beginning to beat and ache between her thighs.

Gianni wrenched back from her to dispose of the remainder of his clothing. Milly opened passion-glazed eyes. She was trembling, her whole body just one gigantic pleading ache. 'Gianni…*please*…' She didn't even know where the words came from.

'It hurts to want this much, doesn't it?' Gianni leant over her, his long, lean body golden and tight with leashed power in the lamplight. His brilliant eyes savoured her quivering tension, watched her look at him with wonder.

'Yes…' It hurt like a knot tightening and tightening inside

her. Her spellbound gaze roamed down over his powerful frame, lingering in sensual shock on the aggressive masculine thrust of his virility. Her mouth ran dry and it was like something unlocked inside her, loosing a hot flood of honey to pool heavily at the very heart of her.

All conquering male, Gianni pulled her close. Then he stared down into her hectically flushed face, his spectacular bone structure ferociously taut, his bright eyes curiously chilling, his beautiful shaped mouth hardening. 'We always connected best at this level, *cara mia.*'

Something in that dark sardonic drawl spooked her, but before she could try to identify that apprehensive dart of unease Gianni eased her slender thighs apart and began to explore her wildly sensitive flesh. Her body jack-knifed under that surge of almost intolerable pleasure. It was mindless, all-encompassing, and she craved its continuance with every tortured and sobbing breath she drew.

But it was still a surprise when Gianni came over her, sinking rough, impatient hands beneath her squirming hips. And suddenly he was there, where the ache was worst, entering her in one powerful thrust that made her cry out.

Excited beyond belief by him, Milly clashed with the charged darkness of his eyes. 'Gianni...?' she gasped.

'*Madre di Dio*...I have to black out *my* memory to do this!' Gianni gritted savagely, driving into her again, making her tender flesh yield more fully to enclose him.

And even as she struggled to comprehend what was wrong, what he meant, the primitive rhythm of his possession engulfed a body too long starved of such sensation. Her confusion was not equal to the overpowering hunger he had awakened. With every driving invasion Gianni sent excitement hurtling through her at storm-force potency. Hot, aching pleasure took her over. Release came in a shattering ecstatic surge that jolted and freed what felt like every fibre of her being.

Within seconds, Gianni hit that same peak with a shuddering groan. Her arms came round him, tears flooding her eyes. That didn't surprise her. It always happened. Sometimes she loved Gianni so much she wanted to scream it from the rooftops, she thought helplessly. She pressed her lips adoringly to a satin-smooth shoulder damp with sweat and whispered it instead.

With startling abruptness he pulled back from her. With a bitten-off Italian curse, he shoved himself away from her. Then he surveyed her with blazing anger and condemnation. 'Bye-bye, Edward, hello, Gianni—all in the space of one day?' he ground out raggedly, strikingly pale beneath his naturally dark skin. 'What sort of a fool do you take me for?'

And Milly went into deep shock then. The cloaking, blinding veil of physical satiation was torn from her mind and dissipated as though it had never been. Every scrap of colour drained from her stricken face as she stared at Gianni, and she stared at him and registered that both past and present now existed in a seamless joining inside her head.

Gianni snatched in a shuddering breath. 'OK...you didn't mean to say it and I overreacted,' he conceded, a slight tremor interfering with his usually even diction, his Sicilian accent very strong.

Sicilian to the backbone, Milly recalled absently, locked into the terrifying enormity of the memories hitting her now from all sides.

'Stop looking at me like that,' Gianni told her.

He thinks he's going to have to apologise, and he hates apologising, so he's digging himself into a deeper hole because when he's really upset about anything he will go to enormous lengths not to confront that reality. All the strength in Milly's body just seeped away as she completed that instant appraisal. She was immobilised by what had happened inside her own head. She had finally got her memory back. Now the shock was telling.

'Milly...' Gianni sat up, dark, deep flashing eyes narrowing on her anguished face and the distance in her eyes. A distance which suggested that though she might appear to be looking at him, for some reason he wasn't really registering.

Gianni, the love of her life, Milly labelled him, in a growing haze of emotional agony. Walking away, acknowledging defeat, had been like driving a knife into her own heart.

'You *hate* me...' she framed sickly, shaking her head back and forth on the pillow in urgent negative, soundless tears beginning to track down her cheeks. 'You *touched* me, hating me!'

Gianni was stunned.

'And how do I know that?' Milly gulped strickenly. 'I know that because I can remember *everything*—but I don't want to...I don't want to remember!' she lashed at him in passionate pain.

Gianni laid Milly down on the great canopied bed in the master suite of his country house—which he had yet to spend a single night in. Back at the hotel, the doctor had given her a sedative, and had then told Gianni in no uncertain terms exactly what he thought of him.

There had been no hiding the fact that that hotel bed had harboured more than one body. With a humility that would have astounded all who knew him, Gianni had withstood being called a selfish swine. At that instant, hovering while Milly shivered and shook with those horrible silent tears, Gianni would have welcomed far stronger censure if it had in any way lessened his own appalling sense of guilt.

He had traumatised her. *Him.* Nobody else. The Jenningses had loved her, and would have protected her while she tried to come to terms with what was happening to her. But he had deliberately severed every tie she had and then quite ruthlessly seduced her back into sexual intimacy. She hadn't been ready for that. She might never have been ready for that again. He had hit on her like a stud when she was weak and confused and scared. She had trustingly turned to him for comfort and he had let his driving need to re-establish a hold on her triumph. He had never sunk so low in his life...

And it was no consolation to know *why* he had done it. Jealousy, bitter and angry, seething up inside him like hot, destructive lava. The thought of Milly loving Benson, wanting him, sleeping with him. Thinking about her with Stefano had been bad enough, but he had learned to block that out. Iron self-discipline had worked for three years. Only it had come apart at the seams the instant he'd tried to make love to her again, suddenly terrified for the first time in his life that he might not be able to do it and then acting like an animal in rut. Great footnote, Gianni. The one and only thing that was ever perfect, you blew!

'Not sleeping?' Connor asked, his little face full of hope.

'Not sleeping,' Milly confirmed gruffly as she set aside her breakfast tray and dragged her son down into her arms to tickle him, listening to his delighted chortles with a sudden lightening of her heart. She kissed his soft cheek and ran a fingertip lovingly down over his small nose. 'I gather I've been sleeping *too* long.'

Connor scrambled down off the bed at speed. Retrieving something from the floor, he clambered back up to show it to her. It was a child's board book. He pointed to the golden-haired princess sleeping on the front cover and said with tremendous pride, 'My mummy!'

As she noted the title, Milly breathed in very deep. *The Sleeping Beauty.* Gianni was very creative in tight corners, and explaining Mummy's sudden need to sleep the clock round and more had evidently not over-taxed his agile brain. Gianni, she reflected tautly, for so long never more than a heartbeat away from her next thought.

Why, oh, why hadn't he just let her stay lost? Connor. But not *only* Connor. Revenge, she decided with a helpless shiver. Revenge as only a Sicilian could enact it. In a reckless drunken attack of lust, Stefano had destroyed them. On his deathbed Gianni wouldn't forgive her for what he believed she'd done to him. And at his coldest Gianni was at his most dangerous. If *only* she had been armoured with the knowledge that she was dealing with a male who hated and despised her when they'd first met again...

But then how many 'if onlys' already littered her history with Gianni? So she had ended up in bed with him again. So she had had a fantastic time. That was the painful crux of the matter, wasn't it? That she had sobbed with ecstasy and clung to a guy who had invaded her eager body with all the rampaging finesse of a stud on a one-night stand!

Gianni, who had taught her that making love could be an art form, Gianni, who was endlessly creative in the bedroom but never, ever rough. Quite deliberately he had set out to use and humiliate her. But it had been the shatteringly sudden return of her memory which had torn her apart. And Gianni was in for a very big surprise if he fondly imagined she was about to greet him with shamed eyes and streaming tears at their next meeting!

But life went on no matter what, Milly told herself with feverish urgency. Gianni was Connor's father now. Nothing more. Her problem was that she needed to learn a whole new way of thinking. Time hadn't passed for her in quite the same way as it had passed for Gianni. Three years ago she had still been hopelessly in love with him. At the instant her memories came alive again she had been engulfed in a devastatingly intense storm of emotion, the most bitter sense of betrayal, loss and anguished pain. Because the man she loved had turned his back on her and walked away. It was those feelings she had to deal with now, and then she had to put them all away again, back where they *really* belonged—in the past.

From her magnificent bed, she surveyed her imposing new surroundings with grudging curiosity, and then, pushing back the fine linen sheet, she got up. When she'd arrived, she had used the bathroom, which had been left helpfully lit with the door ajar. Now that she registered that there were three other doors to choose between she knew why.

Wandering over to one of the tall windows to glance out, she almost tripped over Connor in surprise. Beautiful gardens gave way to rolling fields and distant woodland. She had dimly assumed that she was in a townhouse, hadn't thought to question the lack of traffic noise. Gianni now owned a country home? Gianni, who had once regarded the countryside as the long, boring bit between cities? But then what did she know about Gianni's life these days?

Tensing, she instantly reminded herself that she didn't *want* to know anything! With Connor tagging in her wake she went for a shower, and was drying her hair when a brisk knock sounded on the bedroom door. A youthful brunette peered in, and then flushed when she saw Milly in her bathrobe. 'I'm sorry, Miss Henner. I didn't realise you were up and about. My name's Barbara Withers—'

Connor interrupted her with an exuberant cry of recognition. 'Barb!'

'I'm Connor's temporary nanny. Mr D'Angelo did stress that a permanent appointment would be subject to your approval,' she advanced anxiously.

'Yes...' Conscious of the younger woman's discomfiture, Milly concealed her own disconcertion.

'I was about to offer to take Connor outside to play. Since Mr D'Angelo left him with you after breakfast, I thought you might be tired now,' Barbara explained.

So Connor hadn't wandered into her bedroom under his own steam. Milly had been concerned that no adult appeared to be in charge of him. But it seemed that Gianni had sneakily fed their son in through the door without making a personal appearance. But then with Connor around perhaps that had been a wise decision, and she didn't want him present when she saw Gianni again.

'I'm sure Connor would enjoy that.' Milly's smile was strained by the thought of what lay ahead of her. And that was facing up to the male who, after that dreadful night three years ago, had refused to meet her again, accept her phone calls or answer her letters. Closure had not been a problem for Gianni. He had judged her, dumped her, and replaced her at spectacular speed.

Suddenly cold inside herself, Milly leafed through the garments she had found unpacked in the adjoining dressing room. She had a curious aversion to wearing the clothes she had worn as Faith Jennings, but she had nothing else available. With regret she recalled the wonderful wardrobe she had loftily chosen to leave behind when she had left Paris three years earlier.

In the end she pulled on a pair of faded jeans she had used for gardening and a long-sleeved black polo shirt. Leaving her tumbling mass of golden hair loose round her shoulders, she set off in search of Gianni.

She emerged onto a huge galleried landing dominated by superb oil paintings. For 'country house' she now substituted 'stately home'. The stamp of Gianni's ownership was everywhere. The most magnificent furniture, the most exquisite artwork. He surrounded himself with beautiful possessions and he had fabulous taste and considerable knowledge, all acquired as an adult.

An extraordinary man, she conceded reluctantly. Always a target for the paparazzi, rarely out of the newspapers, inevitably a focus of fascination for others. Precious few men rose to Gianni's level from a deprived and brutalised childhood. A drunken, abusive father, a prostitute mother who had abandoned him, followed by a stepmother who had fed him alongside the dog and chucked him out on the streets of Palermo to fend for himself at the age of ten. Why was she remembering all that? she asked herself angrily.

But all of a sudden it was as if a dam had broken its banks inside Milly's subconscious: memories gushed out against her volition, demanding her attention, refusing to go away…

The year Milly had turned nineteen her life had changed out of all recognition. Leo, her feckless but very charming father, had died of a sudden heart attack in Spain.

After eleven years of sharing her father's gypsy lifestyle,

Milly had wanted to put down roots and make plans. She had applied for a place on a two-year horticultural course at a London college. With not a single educational qualification to her name it had taken courage to put herself forward, and she had been overjoyed when she'd been accepted as a full-time student.

She had lived on a shoestring in a dingy bedsit, working part-time in a supermarket to supplement her tiny grant. Her first real friend had been the bubbly blonde who'd lived across the landing. Lisa had worked for a strippergram agency and had lived in considerably greater comfort than Milly.

One afternoon, Lisa had come to her door in a real state. 'I have to do a booking in the City tonight and I can't make it,' she groaned. 'Stevie's just called to ask me out to dinner and you *know* what he's like! If I'm not available, he'll ask someone else!'

Lisa had given her heart to a real creep. The saga of her sufferings at Stevie's ruthlessly selfish hands could have filled a book the size of the Bible. Yet when Stevie called Lisa still dropped everything and ran, because he had trained her that way.

'Please do this booking for me,' Lisa pleaded frantically. 'You don't have to take *anything* off. All you've got to do is jump out of this stupid fake cake dressed as an angel and smile!'

Milly grimaced. Lisa raced back to her bedsit and returned with an armful of celestial white robes and a small gilded harp. 'It's a really dated stunt, but these executive-types want something tasteful because they're scared witless of offending the big boss. It's his birthday and his name is D'Angelo...*angel*—get it?'

So that was how Milly had ended up jumping out of Gianni's birthday cake. She had thrown herself upright and found herself looking straight down into dark eyes that flashed to the most amazing shade of gold. Those eyes had spooked her. Tripping in her oversized robes, she had lurched off the trolley, careened into the board table beside it to send half the drinks flying and had finally landed in a tumbled heap at Gianni's feet. The ghastly silence her clumsiness had evoked remained with her even now.

'Happy birthday, Mr D'Angelo,' she had muttered doggedly.

'What do you do for an encore?' Gianni enquired in silken enquiry. 'Level the building?'

Severe embarrassment flipped into sudden fury at that sarcastic sally. 'Don't be such an insensitive prat!' Milly hissed in angry reproach. 'Go on—help me up...don't you have any manners at all?'

A swelling tide of gasps, sharp, indrawn breaths and muted groans rose from the executives still glued to their seats round the board table.

Gianni looked stunned. Then, disorientatingly, he threw back his arrogant dark head and laughed. 'For a little titchy thing, you've got quite a tongue, haven't you?'

'You are one ignorant pig!' Milly told him, even as he extended a lean hand to help her upright. She pushed his hand away and sat carefully untangling the robes from her legs so that she could rise without assistance and take a step back to impose some distance between them.

Gianni then helpfully extended the harp she had dropped on him. 'What do you do next?' he asked, lounging back in his imposing chair with an air of sardonic anticipation.

Milly snatched the harp back. 'If you're hoping I'm about to start stripping, it's not your day! I keep all my clothes on.'

Gianni studied her with even greater amusement. 'Aren't you supposed to at least *sing* many happy returns?'

At that reminder, Milly stiffened resentfully. 'I couldn't hold a tune in a bucket.'

'You...are...priceless.' Gianni savoured her, brilliant eyes fixed like lasers to her expressive face.

Rising from his chair to his full intimidating height, Gianni closed one hand over hers and turned to address their gaping audience. 'Check the Health and Safety rules next time you decide to give me a surprise. This particular angel could have sued the pants off us if she'd been hurt!'

'Let go of my hand,' Milly urged as he carried her across the room with him.

He thrust open the door that led back into the corridor. 'Was this your last booking?'

'My only one—'

'Then I'll take you home.'

'No thanks.' Pulling free of his hold, Milly hurried back to the cloakroom in which she had earlier changed out of her own clothes.

When she emerged, clad in jeans and a sweater, Gianni was still waiting for her.

'You're a bit like a dog with a bone, aren't you?'

'You're very beautiful. Don't act so surprised when I tell you that. It doesn't wash with looks like yours,' Gianni drawled with a cynical smile. 'I'll take you home. You can get dressed up. We'll go out to dinner.'

'No, thanks,' she said tautly, annoyed that temptation was flickering when he was so screamingly unsuitable. Dressed up? Dressed up in *what*? Did he think she had a designer wardrobe to fall back on?

'Why not?'

'How many reasons do you need?'

'This is very entertaining. Feel free to speak your mind.'

'All right. One, you're too slick for me. Two, you look filthy rich. Three, you have to be at least ten years older than me, and I can't imagine that we'd have a single thing in common.'

'Are you always this...sharp-tongued?'

She picked up on the deliberate hesitation, recognised the coolness that had quenched the vibrancy in his extraordinary eyes and felt herself shrivel up inside, but still she said, 'No, you bring out the best in me.'

'Instant loathing?'

She shivered, and then, ashamed of her disturbingly unfamiliar need to continually attack him, she decided to be honest. 'No, I fancied you like mad the minute I laid eyes on you, but it's not something I want to follow up,' she admitted, suddenly finding herself alarmingly short of breath. 'Bye. Have a nice birthday!'

The following afternoon, Gianni was waiting for her to come home from college. Having tripped over him on the landing, Lisa was bending over backwards to entertain him in Milly's absence.

'How on earth did you find out where I lived?'

'Bribed the sleazebag who owns the strippergram agency. He told me your name was Lisa. Then I met Lisa and she explained who you *really* were.' Gianni angled a slanting smile over her—a smile that had megawatt charisma.

'You shouldn't have come here—'

'*Dio mio*...what did you expect? You think I'm about to walk in the opposite direction when you're feeling the same way I feel?'

'Tell me one thing we have in common?' Milly invited.

'Sex.'

'When you think of something else, I'll have dinner with you,' Milly told him, hot-cheeked.

Gianni stuck a swift foot in the door she was trying to close on him. 'Quick tempers.'

'You are *so* persistent!'

'OK.' Strong jawline squaring, he shrugged with eye-catching elegance. 'I'm out of here.'

She let him get as far as the floor below, and then, stabbed by the sudden realisation that she would never see him again, she darted back out to the landing and hung over the banister to call, 'Just dinner...all right?'

'What about breakfast?' Gianni asked without hesitation.

'No chance, but I appreciate you being this honest about your intentions. Honesty is very important to me, even if the truth isn't always welcome. So I should tell you now that I'm not into casual sex and I'm very romantic.'

Gianni sighed softly. 'One of us is set to crash into a solid brick wall.'

'It won't be me,' Milly told him gently. 'I couldn't possibly fall in love with someone like you.'

'*Accidenti*…why would I *want* you to fall in love with me?' Gianni demanded incredulously. 'My sole interest in you is—'

'Shut up before you talk yourself out of a dinner date,' Milly advised.

Emerging from the frighteningly fresh hold of those memories back into the present, Milly blinked and looked around herself. She was still standing on the gallery. Breathing in deep, shaken by the tremendous pull of the past, she walked slowly towards the stairs.

As she descended the sweeping staircase Gianni strode out into the wonderful Georgian hall below. Instantly she felt her tender heart quake like a stupid jelly, as if three years hadn't passed, as if her brain was forever locked in time, incapable of moving on and healing. As she stilled two steps up from the foot of the stairs, so that for once she was at his level, her hands closed into defensive fists by her sides.

CHAPTER SEVEN

'GIANNI...' Milly breathed, and she could hardly get his name past her dry lips.

'You don't look at all well,' Gianni drawled with measured cool, incisive dark eyes resting on her without any perceptible expression. 'You really should have stayed in bed.'

Yes, he could have handled her best as a total invalid, Milly decided. Then she would have been an object of pity, too weak and pathetic to require confrontation. Gianni went to quite incredible lengths to avoid emotional scenes. He could not bear to be vulnerable. He could not tolerate any loss of control. So he attached himself to objects, not to people. Perhaps Connor would teach him to love. She had failed—oh, boy, had she failed...

'I'm fine,' she lied, terrified that he was registering just how much he could still affect her.

Gianni looked back at her. She was so small, so slender, so pale, haunted eyes fixed to him as if he was about to unfurl a set of cloven hooves and a toasting fork. *Fine?* The fear she couldn't hide filled him with seething bitterness.

Suddenly he wished her memory had stayed lost. Memories were bloody painful afflictions! That night in the hotel she had been so sweet. Trusting, open, just as he remembered her. The only person alive who had ever treated him as if he was just an ordinary guy. Nagging him when he was late, complaining when he was preoccupied, yawning through the business news and totally forgetting about him when she was out in her precious garden. In every way she had been different from every other woman he had had, either before or since.

110

Once she would have filled this awful silence, instinctively understanding that he couldn't, that when he was wound up about something he turned cold and aggressive and silent in self-defence. Then he reminded himself that this bit would be over soon. Not for nothing had he spent the past twenty-four hours seeking a rational solution to the mess they were in. And around dawn, he had come up with the answer.

Not perfect, but simple. And the instant he made that proposal Milly would go back to normal—well, maybe not immediately, he conceded grudgingly, but *obviously* she'd be over the moon. He'd also have the tactical advantage of surprise. She'd appreciate that he was making a really huge and stupendously generous effort for Connor's sake. And naturally she'd be grateful. Grateful enough to go back upstairs with him and consolidate their new understanding in the most logical way of all?

Milly knew she was gaping at Gianni like a pheasant looking up the barrel of a shotgun. But the lurch of her heart had appalled her. Feeling that sensitive to dark, deep flashing eyes as chilly as a winter's day was not a good sign. Noticing that he looked shockingly spectacular in a casual designer suit the colour of caramel was an even worse sign. Say something, a voice in her head screeched, for heaven's sake, *say* something. But her mind was a complete blank. She didn't know where to start or how she would ever stop if she did start. Silence seemed a lot safer.

Milly stiffened as Gianni extended a hand to her. It was the very last gesture she had expected from him. Uncurling her fingers, she lifted her arm in slow motion. He got tired waiting. He brought up his other hand, closed both round her waist and lifted her down to the marble-tiled floor.

A slight gasp of disconcertion escaped her. However, the sudden shrinkage in stature she suffered helped. Suddenly her strained eyes were mercifully level with Gianni's chest.

'We've got some talking to do,' Gianni informed her next. Milly was poleaxed. Only a woman who had been intimately involved with Gianni could have understood that acknowledgement to be ground-breaking and incredible. Whenever she had wanted to talk, seriously talk about personal things, Gianni had had a hundred evasive techniques. 'Later' had been a particular favourite, followed by a sudden rampant desire for her body or a pressing appointment. It had taken her a very long time to appreciate that 'later' meant never.

'A lot...' Milly agreed breathlessly, suddenly experiencing a stark, shameful stab of pained resentment. What had changed Gianni? *Who* had changed him? Who had finally persuaded him that honest communication was the only option when the going got tough? It was what they had once so badly needed, but the offer was coming way too late for her to benefit.

He showed her into a library, where a log fire was burning in the grate. He strode over to the desk, lifted the phone and ordered coffee. Stilling by the hearth, Milly stretched her unsteady hands out to the heat and let her gaze travel around the magnificent room with its warm red décor.

'What do you think of Heywood House?' Gianni asked.

'It's beautiful.' She resisted the urge to admit that it wasn't at all what she had expected. She didn't want to stray onto impersonal topics and deflect him from anything he might want to say to her.

'The gardens are famous. I've ensured that they've been maintained to the highest standards,' Gianni advanced smoothly.

Milly wandered over to the nearest window. She adored gardens, but right now she was so enervated she couldn't even appreciate the wonderful view. 'It looks tremendous.'

'There's a rare plant centre attached to the estate. I rebuilt it,' Gianni continued. 'It doesn't exactly do a roaring trade, but the manager tells me it's a real haunt for the connoisseur.

Bewildered by this flood of extraneous information from a male who barely knew the difference between a rose and a daisy and was content to remain in a state of blissful ignorance, Milly suddenly frowned as her mind homed in on something else entirely, and she exclaimed, 'For goodness' sake, Gianni...I haven't even spoken to Louise! What on earth must she be thinking? She's my partner and my best friend and I didn't even *phone* her!'

The silence spread and spread.

Gianni dealt her a fulminating look. 'I phoned her. She was very concerned. I said you'd be in touch when you were well enough...OK?'

Milly released her breath, relieved by that assurance. But she wondered why he had delivered the news with such an air of impatience. It wasn't as if she had interrupted him when he'd been talking about anything important. The door opened and a maid entered with a tray of coffee. It was a welcome diversion.

She sat down in a leather wing-back armchair and poured the coffee. Without hesitation she added three sugars to Gianni's cup.

'We'll deal with practicalities first, get them out of the way,' Gianni announced with decisive cool. 'And naturally the first thing I want to know is, have you any idea who left you lying badly injured on that road in Cornwall? And how did it happen?'

Milly jerked and froze, her heartbeat thudding loudly in her ears. Such obvious questions. Why hadn't she been prepared for them?

'It must be distressing for you to have to remember that night. But it has to be dealt with.' Gianni watched her with keen, dark expectant eyes.

Milly was shot right back to that night, forced to recall things she would have preferred to leave buried, things that had nothing whatsoever to do with the accident. She lost colour. Her hand began to shake. She set down her coffee again with a clatter. She hoped to heaven Gianni didn't ask her what she had been *doing* in Cornwall in the first place, because if he did ask, she certainly didn't feel like telling him the truth.

'Milly...?' Gianni pressed, more gently. 'Do you remember what happened now?'

'M-mostly...not very clearly.' A taxi had dropped her off at the cottage where Stefano had been staying with his girlfriend. She had forgotten to ask the taxi driver to wait for her: a very foolish oversight. But it had taken a lot of courage to seek out and confront Stefano. And when she had walked back out of that cottage she had felt dead inside and she really hadn't cared about anything. Not the darkness, not the wind, not the rain. She had just started walking away as fast as she could.

'I got lost,' Milly muttered tightly.

'Where was this? Why were you were on foot?'

'I'd gone visiting...and, coming back, I messed up my transport arrangements. So was walking,' she began afresh, staring blindly at the silver sugar bowl, determined not to tell him any actual lies. 'It was a horrible wet night.'

Gianni bent down, closed a hand over her knotted fingers and eased her slowly upright into the circle of his arms. 'It was also a long time ago, *cara*. It can't hurt you now.'

Helplessly, Milly leant into him for support, but she felt like a fraud. 'There really isn't much to remember, Gianni. I *think* I may have heard the car that hit me approaching but that's it. There's nothing else. I don't recall seeing a car or being hit.' She bowed her damp brow against his chest. 'What has always given me the creeps is the knowledge that somebody robbed me while I was lying there hurt. I had an overnight bag with me.'

'The hit-and-run driver and the thief may well have been the same person,' Gianni ground out, and she could feel the massive restraint he was exerting over his anger on her behalf. The knowledge of that anger comforted her. 'I'm afraid the police will be hoping for more details than you've been able to give me.'

'The police?' Milly echoed in surprise.

'Some bastard left you lying by the side of that road like a piece of rubbish!' Gianni reminded her with barely suppressed savagery. 'You'd be dead if a passing motorist hadn't seen you and contacted the emergency services. It's a complete miracle that you didn't have a miscarriage!'

Milly sighed. 'I don't really want to talk to the police about this again.'

Gianni veiled his gaze. 'You'll have to make a new statement, but I can understand that you don't like the idea of it all being raked up again,' he conceded soothingly as he settled her back into the wing-back chair. 'I've still got a few questions I'd like answered, but we'll leave them for now.'

'Yes…' Milly averted her pounding head, stomach still churning. She really didn't want Gianni to know she'd gone to see Stefano. She knew what interpretation he would put on that revelation. And Stefano had clearly known better than to ever mention her visit. That was no surprise to her. Gianni's kid brother had treated her like Typhoid Mary that night. With great difficulty, Milly put away that memory.

'Right,' Gianni breathed in a next-on-the-agenda tone, as if he was chairing a board meeting. 'I imagine you'd like to know where we're heading now.'

Considering that in two entire years with her Gianni had not once even hinted that they might be heading anywhere beyond his next flying visit, Milly was taken aback by that concise assurance. She looked up, sapphire-blue eyes very wide and wary.

Gianni leant back against his desk, looking incredibly sophisticated and elegant in his unstructured caramel suit and black T-shirt. Milly averted her head again and rubbed at a worn seam on her jeans with restive fingers.

'To start with I should tell you why I bought this place two years ago.'

Milly frowned, not understanding why that should be of interest to her.

'Heywood House is convenient both to the airport and the City of London. I hoped that once I found you both, you would move in here—'

'Move in here?' Milly glanced up in frank bewilderment. *'Why?'*

Gianni sighed, as if she was being incredibly slow on the uptake. 'Naturally I want you to live at a location where I can easily maintain regular contact with Connor. Heywood House fits the bill very well.'

'Two years ago, you purchased this property for *me*?' Milly was thinking out loud, and she flushed with embarrassment when reality sank in a split second later.

Gianni had bought a stately home and turned it into a treasure house. Naturally *not* for her benefit but for his child's! Even that far back Gianni had been making plans. Selecting the kind of home he wanted his child to grow up in, filling it with priceless artwork and furniture to create a gilded cocoon of wealth and privilege. Could she ever have dreamt three years ago that he would warm to the concept of being a father to such an extent? With an effort, she forced her attention back to him.

'To all intents and purposes Heywood House *will* be yours, until Connor reaches his twenty-fifth birthday.' Gianni made that distinction with complete cool. 'I intend to sign all the documentation to that effect and this is now your home. I want you to feel secure here.'

Everything to be tied up all nice and tight and legal. Very much Gianni's stamp. Gianni had already worked out how best to control her and, through her, his child. Where they lived, *how* they lived. And, to that end, Heywood House would be put in trust for their son. Milly stared down into her untouched coffee, feeling incredibly hurt and humiliated. He didn't trust her as far as he could throw her now—but then had he ever?

For the first time since she had recovered her memory, Milly recalled the DNA testing Gianni had mentioned. A shudder of very real repulsion ran through her in response. One glimpse of her with Stefano and that had been that. Instantly Gianni had been willing to believe her capable of any evil. Two years of her loving faith had been eradicated in a nano-second. Now, it seemed, he didn't even trust her not to try and make a claim for a share of this house at some time in the future.

'I thought you'd be pleased about the gardens and the plant centre.' Gianni regarded her like a generous benefactor, still awaiting the gratitude he saw as his due and keen to give her a helpful nudge in the right direction. 'Obviously those factors influenced my choice of this particular property.'

Unable to credit that, hating her as he did, he could have been influenced by any desire to please her, Milly swallowed hard. 'Didn't it occur to you that I might want to live somewhere of my *own* choosing?'

'Within certain parameters,' Gianni qualified without hesitation. 'This is my son we're talking about, but let's put that issue aside for now. I have something far more important I want to discuss with you...'

A slightly jagged laugh escaped Milly's tight, dry throat. Her nerves were already stretched tight as piano wires.

'What's so funny?' Gianni asked.

'Once, whenever I said anything like that to you, it really used to spook you,' Milly reminded him helplessly.

His lean, dark features clenched hard, the dark, deep flashing eyes chilling to polar ice. '"Once" is not a barrier we want to cross. I don't want to rake over the past.'

The sudden freeze in the atmosphere raised goosebumps on Milly's over-sensitive skin. She tore her strained and shadowed gaze away. She got the message. Three years ago he had denied her the chance to give her version of what happened the night he had found her with Stefano. And now he was telling her that she would never get that chance. *Never, ever.* Only Gianni, so practised at keeping unpleasant or awkward things in tight little separate compartments, could fondly imagine it possible for her to respect such an embargo.

'For Connor's sake, we *need* to move on,' Gianni added with cool emphasis.

Honest communication? Why on earth had she got her hopes up? They were to move on without ever having paused to consider. Gianni hadn't changed one iota. And Gianni was far too proud to confront an episode that had undoubtedly savaged his ego. So their entire past had now become a conversational no-go area. *For Connor's sake.* That phrase had an almost pious ring of superiority. Naturally it did. Gianni thought Connor's mother was the immoral slut who had lured his kid brother into bed with her.

'I'd like my son to have my name,' Gianni admitted.

Milly raised dulled eyes, wishing he could look ugly to her just once, wishing his flaws would shriek at her loud enough to destroy the dangerous emotions swilling about inside her. But, no, Gianni lounged back against that desk looking drop-dead gorgeous, relaxed and in spectacular control of the situation.

Milly rose to her feet. She parted her lips, and with a defiance she could not withstand breathed raggedly, 'Your brother assaulted me.'

Gianni froze. A kind of incredulous outrage laced with black fury flared in his brilliant eyes.

'Just thought you should know,' Milly completed shakily.

'Keep quiet...' All cool ditched, Gianni studied her with glittering rage and derision, every line of his big, powerful body poised like a predator about to spring. 'I won't listen to your lies. I will not discuss this with you, *capisce*? One more word and I walk out of this room—'

'Go ahead.' Milly stood her ground. Indeed, all of a sudden she felt as if she was wedged in concrete, ready to hold steady through any storm.

'And I head straight for my lawyers and I throw everything I've got at you and fight for custody of Connor!'

Milly's stomach lurched as suddenly as if Gianni had thrown her off a cliff. White as milk, she gazed back at him in horror.

'Now you've got the message,' Gianni murmured grittily, his anger back under lock and key as he recognised her response.

The shock of that unashamed threat savaged Milly. And suddenly she couldn't bear to look at him any longer. She was too damned scared of him. Scared of Gianni for the first time in her life. Before, she had only feared his hold on her emotions. Now she feared a whole lot of other things as well. His innate ruthlessness, his enormous wealth, the dangerous power and influence he had at his fingertips.

She was shaking, and she hated that he should see that. But she didn't need a crystal ball to guess the sort of weapons which might be used against her in any custody battle. A woman capable of spending three years living another woman's life might well fail to impress a judge as a stable mother figure. In fact, her recent past would put her at a distinct disadvantage, Milly reflected bitterly.

'But I wouldn't do that, to you or Connor. I think you're a great mother. I have no intention of trying to take him away from you. OK?' Gianni breathed tautly.

Her arms protectively wrapped around herself and her back turned to him, Milly continued to stare blindly out of the window. His words meant nothing to her. She knew she would never forget the way Gianni had just turned on her. His façade of civilised cool and control had dropped to let her see the cold menace that still lay beneath. Why was she so shocked? Hadn't she always known that Gianni was totally incapable of forgiving her for what he believed she had done?

'I suppose I should've expected you to come out with that sort of stuff today,' Gianni continued flatly. 'But you have to accept that I've put all that behind me.'

Her supposed betrayal. Like a gun he concealed behind his back, always primed to shoot.

'To the extent…' Unusually, Gianni hesitated. 'You've really messed this moment up, Milly.'

'What moment?' she muttered in confusion.

'I was about to ask you to marry me. *Accidenti*, I *am* asking you to marry me!' Gianni rephrased, with more than a suggestion of gritted teeth.

Milly went from shock into bigger, deeper shock. She had to consciously will her feet to turn around so that she could look at him again. She *had* to look at him to believe the evidence of her own ears.

A dark line of colour accentuating his stunning cheekbones, Gianni subjected her to a grim, glittering appraisal. 'In spite of everything you've done, I'm willing to give you another chance and make you my wife.'

'Wife...' Milly could hardly get her tongue round that astounding word. 'But you hate me...'

Gianni raised two lean brown hands and spread them at truly impressive speed to indicate his distaste for that subject. 'I don't want to get into emotions here. They're quite irrelevant.'

'Irrelevant...' Milly stared at him with huge wondering eyes.

'All that really matters is that you're the mother of my son. Connor deserves a proper family life and he's not going to get that if I'm just the guy who flies in to visit every week,' Gianni pointed out levelly. 'I want to be a real father. I don't want him turning round and asking me as a teenager why I never thought enough of him to marry his mother and be a genuine part of his life.'

Milly nodded in slow motion.

'Then there's us,' Gianni added in an obvious afterthought. 'Let's be frank, *cara*. You wouldn't kick me out of bed.'

Hot, humiliated colour drenching her former pallor, Milly discovered that she wanted to kick him to kingdom come.

'I don't see any reason why things shouldn't go right back to the way they were,' Gianni told her with complete conviction. 'I still find it a real challenge to keep my hands off you."

'That's a...a compliment?' Milly prompted unevenly.

Gianni slanted an ebony brow. 'I'm asking you to marry me. I can understand that you're pretty surprised by this development, but you should be really pleased.'

'Why?'

'Why?' Gianni repeated with unconcealed incredulity. 'It's what you always secretly wanted. Do you think I didn't realise that?'

Kicking him to kingdom come wouldn't be enough. It would be too quick, too clean. Milly wanted him stretched on a rack and tortured. How could a male so very clever make a marriage proposal sound so deeply offensive? It *had* to be deliberate. He had decided he had to marry her for Connor's sake, but he was making it brutally clear that his sole use for her would be sexual. Connor deserved a relationship; she didn't.

Gianni surveyed Milly's frozen little face with mounting tension. He could feel his temper rising again, no matter how hard he tried to ram it down. Wasn't she capable of a logical reaction? First she had wrecked everything by actually daring to refer to that disgusting episode with Stefano. Next she had told stupid lies. And now she was reacting to his extraordinarily generous proposal as if he had insulted her beyond belief!

Here he was, striving in the only way he could to make amends for his own errors of judgement over the past few days! He was giving her what she must always have wanted when she least deserved it, but not one ounce of appreciation was he receiving for his impressive ability to rise above *her* unforgivable act of betrayal three years ago! And, finally, he had been *honest* with her, Gianni reflected with smouldering resentment. Right from the instant he had first met her, she had stressed how important it was that he should always be honest with her. So he had been honest. Only somehow honesty wasn't working like any magic charm!

'You said that to all intents and purposes this is my home,' Milly reminded him tightly.

'What's that got to do with anything?' Gianni demanded with stark impatience, brilliant eyes glittering like ice shards.

'If this *is* my home, I can ask you to get out of it,' Milly informed him, her breath catching audibly in her throat. 'So I'm asking…'

Gianni frowned at her. 'Run that by me again.'

Milly thrust up her chin. 'In fact, I'm not asking. I'm *telling* you to get out!'

Wrathful incredulity emanated from Gianni in powerful waves. His eyes flashed shimmering gold. 'How *dare* you talk to me like that?'

Milly's temper rose hot enough to equal his own. She took a step forward. 'You're complaining about how *I'm* talking to *you*? You dragged me back into bed at the hotel just so that you could satisfy yourself that you could still pull me like a Christmas cracker!'

'*Dio*…how can you be so vulgar?' Gianni shot at her thunderously.

'Vulgar? *Me?*' Milly gasped in disbelief. 'Would you listen to yourself? You're the cockroach who had to boast about the fact that I *didn't* have the wit to kick you out of bed! Well, now that I've got my memory back, I know I'd sooner be dead than let you touch me again!'

'Is that a fact?' Before she could even guess his intention, Gianni reached out and simply lifted her up into his powerful arms as if she were a doll.

'Put me down this minute!' Milly shrieked at him furiously.

His mouth slammed down on hers like a silencer. Rage hurtled up inside her, only to be transformed into a blaze of white-hot hunger so intense it literally hurt. It physically hurt to want, to need, to crave to such an extent, for nothing he could do could ever be enough. She always wanted more. The drugging heat of his mouth, the provocative stab of his tongue driving her wild only made her ache unbearably for the fulfilment that he alone could give. Heartbeat pounding, pulses racing, she dug her fingers into his luxuriant hair and kissed him back so frantically she couldn't even stop to breathe.

Gianni dragged his mouth off hers. He was breathing heavily, but his dark golden eyes shimmered with unashamed satisfaction. 'Somehow I don't think death before dishonour is likely to figure in this reconciliation, *cara mia*.'

The raging fire within Milly shrank to a tiny mortified flicker and was doused entirely by an all-consuming ache of regret. Her cheeks a hectic pink, she removed her fingers shakily from his hair, tormented by her own weakness.

Gianni lowered her to the carpet again with exaggerated care.

Immediately she spun away in a jerky movement. 'Go, Gianni,' she urged in desperation.

'Call me when you've thought things over,' he murmured silkily, all cool now restored.

Milly listened to the quiet thud of the door closing on his exit and slumped, bitterly ashamed of her own behaviour. He had levelled the score. He had had the last word. Although, as usual, language hadn't played much part in her defeat. But it hadn't always been like that between them, she reminded herself fiercely. Once she *had* been strong enough to hang onto her pride and independence and protect herself from a male determined not to commit himself...

Five years ago, on the very first day they met and admitted to diametrically opposed expectations, Gianni had accurately forecast that *one* of them was set to crash into a solid brick wall.

Gianni had wanted a no-strings-attached affair, but Milly had wanted and needed something much deeper. Within the first week, she had recognised the disturbing intensity of her own emotional response to him. And the discovery that one kiss could set a bushfire burning inside her had been no more welcome.

Milly had tried to back off and protect herself by making loads of rules to ensure that she never emulated poor Lisa with Stevie. No man was going to turn *her* into a puppet on a string! So, if Gianni hadn't called far enough in advance, she'd always been busy. If Gianni had just turned up without calling, she'd always been on the way out of the door to a pressing engagement. If Gianni had been late, she'd gone out and stayed out. And she had never, ever called him.

But then Gianni had gone over to New York for three weeks, and her whole world had turned gloomy grey. She'd begun marking off days on the calendar, hanging over the phone anxiously, and driving herself crazy with the suspicion that he might have other women in his life.

'Have you?' Milly had asked baldly, the first time she'd seen him again.

'Of course I have,' Gianni admitted without hesitation. 'I travel a great deal. Anything else would be impractical.'

Feeling as if she had been slugged by a sack of coal, Milly cleared her throat. 'But if we have an affair, that would change...wouldn't it?' she almost whispered.

Gianni lifted one broad shoulder in an infinitesimal shrug, too slick an operator to be entrapped by a verbal response.

But Milly had got her answer in that silence. And, having naively assumed that even Gianni would concede that intimacy should be accompanied by total fidelity, she was shocked and furious. 'All I can say is, thank heaven I found this out before I slept with you!' she slung as she rose from her seat and stalked out of the restaurant.

'I don't like public scenes. Nor do I admire jealous, possessive women,' Gianni imparted chillingly, outside on the pavement.

'Then what are you doing with me?' Milly demanded. 'I'm jealous and I'm *very* possessive, so get out of my life now and don't come back!'

Gianni stayed away another full month.

Milly lost a stone in weight, but she didn't wait by the phone; she didn't ever expect to see him again. But Gianni was waiting for her to come home one evening when she finished her supermarket shift.

One look and she was sick with simultaneous nerves and sheer, undiluted joy. Gianni took her back to his Park Lane apartment. He dropped the news that she no longer had competition. She asked him how she could be sure of that. Gianni could freely admit that *he* didn't trust anybody, but, faced with her lack of faith in *him*, he was outraged. They almost had another fight.

She was in tears, and then he kissed her—a standard Gianni response when things got too emotional. And the wild passion just blazed up so powerfully inside her she finally surrendered. He was astonished when he realised he was her first lover.

Making love with Gianni was glorious; staying for breakfast feeling totally superfluous while he made calls and read stockmarket reports was something less than glorious.

So Milly drew up a new set of rules. No staying overnight. No asking when she would see him again. Always saying goodbye with a breezy smile. By then, she knew she was in love with him, but she was well aware that he didn't love her. He found her good company. She made him laugh. He couldn't get enough of her in bed. But never once did he do or say anything that gave her any hope that their affair might last.

As part of her college course that year Milly had to spend two months gaining practical experience of working in a large garden or park. She was allotted a place on a big private estate far from London. When she informed Gianni that she would be going away, they had a blistering row.

'How the hell am I supposed to see you up there?' he demanded incredulously.

'You're out of the country at least two weeks out of every four,' she reminded him.

'*Porca miseria*…you can't make a comparison like that!'

'Don't say what you're dying to say,' she warned him tautly. 'It'll make me very angry.'

'I don't know what you're talking about.'

So she said it for him. 'You think your life and your

business empire are one hundred times more important than anything in mine.'

'Obviously they are,' Gianni stated without flinching. 'And, while we're on the subject, I can think of a thousand more suitable career choices than a peculiar desire to go grubbing about in the dirt of somebody else's garden!'

'It's what I want to do. It's what I'll be doing a long, long time after you're gone. So really, in every way, it has to take precedence,' Milly retorted shakily.

'Over *me*?' Gianni breathed chillingly. 'Haven't I offered to find you a decent job?'

'I'm happy with the career choice I'm training for.'

'Fine. Just don't expect me to follow you north to the rural wastes!'

'I never did expect you to. You're far too used to people doing the running for you. You never, ever put yourself out for anybody,' Milly pointed out with quiet dignity. 'So that's that, then. We're at the end of the road.'

'Spare me the clichés at least,' Gianni ground out as she walked straight-backed to the door. 'Tell me, am I being dumped *again*?'

Milly thought about it, and nodded.

'This is a wind-up,' Gianni drawled in icy condemnation. 'This is a power-play.'

'Goodbye,' she said gruffly.

He did come up north. His limo got bogged down in a country lane. He was fit to be tied when he ended up lodged in a very small and far from luxurious hotel. And he was furious when she wouldn't let him come to the estate to pick her up for the weekend. He didn't appreciate being told that she didn't want to shock the head gardener and his wife, who were letting her stay in their guest-room. By the time she had finished explaining that a humble student trainee couldn't have a very rich, flash older boyfriend without her reputation taking a nosedive, and the all too human effect that might have on her receiving a fair assessment of her work, Gianni was not in a very good mood.

'So I'll buy you a big garden of your own,' he announced, in the dark of the night.

'Don't be silly.'

'Then I'll buy the garden for myself. I'll pay you to look after it for me!'

'You're embarrassing me,' she groaned. 'Stop living in fantasy land.'

'When I've got free time, I'd like you to be available *occasionally*.'

'I know how that feels. You're away much more than I am,' she complained sleepily, looking forward to spending two entire nights with him, snuggling up to him with a euphoric smile in the darkness.

'Do you think the head gardener and his wife would be shocked if I delivered you back strangled?' Gianni mused reflectively. 'What am I *doing* here in this lousy dump with you?'

Sex, she reflected. Sex and only sex—and it was an ongoing source of amazement to her that her body could possibly have such a hold on him. It was a perfectly ordinary body. Slender, well-honed, but far from being centrefold material. Yet he kept on coming back to her. She was developing expectations on that basis. That worried her terribly. After all, some day soon he would lose interest and vanish for good.

He came up north three more weekends. She was so happy she couldn't hide it from him. It was getting harder and harder to obey her own rules. It was as if he knew her rules and worked overtime to try and get her to compromise them. That next summer he was away a lot, and she pined, went off her food, couldn't sleep. He gave her a mobile phone and she accepted it, and used it much more than she felt she should.

Then they had their six-month anniversary, and she was stupid enough to mention it. He frowned. 'That long?' he questioned with brooding coolness, and went silent on her for the rest of the evening.

He didn't call her for a week after that. So she called him in a temper and told him he was history and that she was going to find a man who would treat her with the respect she deserved.

'Tell him in advance how demanding you are,' Gianni advised helpfully. 'That you have a very hot temper, a habit of saying things you don't mean and a stubborn streak a mile wide.'

'I'm finished with you—'

'I'll pick you up for dinner at eight, and if you're not there, I'm not waiting. It's time to join the grown-ups and stop playing hard to get.'

Just before she started back at college, she suffered what appeared to be a really bad bout of tonsillitis, and instead of getting better she lost her energy and her appetite. Gianni was in South America. She told him that she thought she had the flu and soldiered on, exhausted, to her classes and her part-time job. By the time Gianni flew back to London she was so weak that walking from the bed to the door was enough to reduce her to a perspiring wreck.

Gianni was furious with her. He got another doctor. Acute glandular fever was diagnosed. She was told she would have to rest for weeks. She wouldn't be fit for her classes or for any other form of work—and by the way, the doctor added, physical intimacy was out for the foreseeable future too. That quickly, her whole world fell apart. At the time she just could not comprehend why Gianni, threatened by weeks of celibacy, should still seem so incredibly supportive.

Forty-eight hours later, she was flown to Paris in Gianni's private jet and installed in a fabulous townhouse with a garden. When she was least able to oppose him Gianni made his move, at supersonic speed.

His every argument had been unanswerable. Who would look after her in London? How could he take care of her from a distance? And she loved Paris, didn't she? If she couldn't study and she couldn't work, she might as well regard her lengthy convalescence as a vacation. And the sad truth was that she was so desperately grateful that Gianni wasn't abandoning her she didn't protest that much.

He was really wonderful when she was ill. She learnt that he liked to be needed, and that in constantly asserting her independence she had been missing out on probably the very best side of him. From that time on, Gianni became the love of her life, the centre of her existence. She stopped trying to contain her own feelings. The last barriers came down. She told him she loved him. He froze, but he didn't back off. The more she told him, the less he froze, and eventually he even began to smile.

And she decided then that maybe if she absolutely showered him in love and trust and affection, if she gave and gave and gave, with complete honesty and generosity, she might break his barriers down too. Her only goal was that he should return her love. So she never did go back to complete her college course.

Gianni became her full-time occupation. He finally got everything the way he wanted. He got to buy her clothes and jewellery, to switch her between the house in Paris and the apartment in New York, according to what best suited his travelling itinerary. She became his mistress full-time without ever acknowledging what she had become. And he was right; she *was* deliriously happy—right up until the day she discovered she was pregnant.

In the heat of passion, Gianni had on several occasions neglected to take precautions. She knew that. *He* knew that. But, like so much else, they had never discussed the fact that he had taken that risk.

Yet the evening she broke the news Gianni went into shock, like a teenager who had honestly believed it couldn't possibly be that easy to get a girl pregnant.

'You can't be…' he said, turning visibly pale beneath his bronzed skin.

'I *am*…no doubt about it. No mistake,' she stressed, getting more and more apprehensive. 'It was that night we—'

'Let's not get bogged down in details,' Gianni interrupted,

striding across the room to help himself to a very large brandy.

'You don't want to talk about this, do you?' she muttered tightly.

'Not right now, no.' Quick glance at gold watch, apologetic look laced with a hint of near desperation.

'You've got some calls to make?'

'No—'

'You have a business meeting at eleven o'clock at night? Well, some celebration this is turning out to be.'

'Celebration?' Gianni awarded her a truly stunned appraisal. 'You're pregnant and we're not married and you want to *celebrate*?'

'Since you're the one who's been playing Russian roulette with my body, maybe you'd like to tell me what end result you expected?'

'I just didn't *think*!' he ground out, like a caged lion, longing to claw at the bars surrounding him, resisting the urge with visible difficulty.

Yet he thought about everything else…incessantly. He thought rings round her. He planned business manoeuvres in his sleep. He was seriously telling her that he hadn't once acknowledged the likely consequences of making love without contraception?

'I'm not having a termination. You might as well know that now,' she whispered sickly.

'*Madre di Dio*…why do you *always* think you know what's on my mind when you don't?' he slashed back at her rawly. 'I don't believe in abortion!'

Only a little of her tension evaporated. 'I'm tired. I'm going to bed.'

'I'm going out.'

'I know.' She closed the door softly, heard the brandy goblet smash and shivered. He was right. So much of the time she did not have one earthly clue what was going on inside him. But that night she believed she did. He might not believe in abortion, but he still didn't want her to have his baby.

The next development shocked her rigid. Gianni walked out of the Paris apartment that night and vanished into thin air for thirty-six hours. He even switched off his mobile phone—an unheard-of development. His security staff went crazy the next morning, questioning her, checking the hospitals, considering kidnapping. They weren't able to accept that Gianni should choose to deliberately take himself off without cancelling his appointments.

Milly convinced herself that he had gone to some other woman.

But Gianni reappeared, looking pale and grim as death, hiding behind an enormous bunch of flowers. And she didn't say a word, behaved as if he had only stepped out an hour earlier. Patently relieved by that low-key reception, Gianni swept her up into his arms and just held her for the first time in his life, so tightly she could barely breathe.

'You just took me by surprise. My own father…if he *was* my father,' he qualified in a roughened undertone. 'He was abusive. I don't know how to be a father, but I don't want to lose you!'

She had never loved Gianni more than she loved him at that moment. It felt like an emotional breakthrough: Gianni trusting her enough to refer to the childhood he never mentioned and actually admitting to self-doubt. Her heart and her hopes soared as high as the sky. Yet, just two short months later, Gianni had almost destroyed her with his lack of his faith…

Coming back to the present to gaze like a wakening sleeper round the library of Heywood House, Milly found that her cheeks were wet with tears. You've got to stop this, she warned herself angrily. There *is* life after Gianni. Three years ago she hadn't felt able to cope with that challenge. But now she was older, wiser…only still as hopelessly in love with him as she had ever been.

CHAPTER EIGHT

'GIANNI...it's me,' Milly announced tautly, her grip so tight on the phone that her knuckles showed white.

'I'm listening,' Gianni responded softly.

'Connor's asking about you all the time.' Milly's troubled eyes were pinned to where her son sat listlessly swinging his feet. 'When I asked you to leave, I overlooked the fact that he's lost a whole life too. The last thing he needs right now is for you to vanish as well—'

'I can be with you in two hours,' Gianni interposed, smooth as silk, but she sensed the buzz of his satisfaction nonetheless. 'Why did you wait four days to contact me?'

Milly tensed. 'I needed some time to myself.'

Before he could ask her what she had decided to do about the marriage question, she finished the call. Then she breathed in very deep to steady herself.

She had lunch with Connor, who could hardly eat for excitement. Leaving him in Barbara's care, she then took herself off outdoors, keen to be elsewhere when Gianni arrived to spend time with their son.

An afternoon spent energetically digging in the walled kitchen garden which had been abandoned to the forces of nature for a good twenty years proved therapeutic. She was going to marry Gianni. *Of course* she was. If he married her, he could hardly use her recent past as a weapon against her in any custody battle. As a wife she would be safer. That way, and only that way, could she ensure that Gianni would find it extremely difficult to try and remove their son from her care.

And if she didn't marry him mightn't he eventually marry someone else? With sudden violence, Milly slashed a bram-

132

ble out of her path. Once she would not have believed that possible. Once she would have sworn that Gianni would die single. But that conviction had died when Gianni had stunned her by proposing. Even if it was only for his son's benefit, Gianni was finally prepared to offer commitment. If Milly turned him down, sooner or later he would end up marrying some other woman.

And that was a development which Milly *knew* she would not be able to bear. She was possessive. She was very possessive. Currently hating and resenting Gianni to the same degree with which she loved him did not blind Milly to her own vulnerability. To stand by on the sidelines and watch Gianni with another woman would be to tear herself to shreds. After all, she reflected painfully, she already knew what that experience felt like. So there was a lot to be said for choosing to be miserable *with* Gianni now that she had faced the fact that she would be even more miserable without him.

'I really love it when you dress up for me like this, *cara*…'

Milly jerked, froze, and then slowly lifted her golden head. Silhouetted against the fading light of the afternoon, Gianni was poised several feet away, a faint smile on his wide, sensual mouth. His navy cashmere coat hung open to reveal a formal pinstripe suit cut to faithfully follow his powerful frame and his long, long legs. He looked spectacular. Her eyes widened, her mouth ran dry, her heart just lurched.

Milly leant on her spade for support. Her tumbled hair was roughly caught back with a piece of twine. She wore ancient jeans, a warm but shapeless sweater and workmanlike boots. Her lack of elegance didn't trouble her. But she could see it was troubling Gianni, who was reading all sorts of deeper messages into her appearance. Women wore make-up in bed with Gianni. Women spent hours dressing to go out with him. He never had known quite how to handle her unconcern at letting him occasionally see her just as she was, bare of both fashion and artifice.

'You lost track of time. You didn't realise I'd arrived,' Gianni decided instantly.

Milly was not in a conciliatory mood. 'I could hardly have missed the helicopter landing, and that was what…two, three hours ago?'

'Your phone is switched off. Barbara Withers told me where to find you.' Gianni couldn't quite conceal his irritation that he had been reduced to asking such a question. 'You shouldn't be working outdoors in this weather.'

'You're annoyed I wasn't waiting for you at the house,' Milly interpreted without the slightest difficulty. 'But why come all the way down here to get an answer you don't need? The last time you were here you made it clear that you saw my answer as a foregone conclusion.'

His lean, strong face darkened, brilliant eyes veiling to reveal only a watchful glimmer of gold.

'*And,*' Milly continued flatly, aiming a particularly vicious jab of the spade at the undergrowth surrounding her, 'as usual you were right. How *can* I say no?'

'You're going to marry me.' Ignoring the hostile undertones with the practised ease of a male who never looked for trouble with a woman unless it rose up and slapped him smack in the face, Gianni surveyed her with a slow smile curling his expressive mouth. He retained his cool like a cloaking device, but his eyes glittered like the heart of a fire.

'But I have certain conditions,' Milly extended gently.

Caught off guard, Gianni strode closer, stepping off the path to mire his polished Italian leather shoes in mud. '*Conditions?*'

Milly threw back her slight shoulders like a boxer about to enter the ring. 'To start with, I'd like you to have a medical, so that I can be assured that you have a completely clean bill of health.'

His winged brows lifted. 'What are you talking about?'

'Whether you choose to believe it or not, I have *not* been

intimate with anybody but you,' Milly stated, watching his strikingly handsome features freeze, his big, powerful body stiffen. 'However, you can't offer me the same reassurance, and I feel I have the right to ask.'

Gianni drew himself up to his full height, dark eyes blazing derision. '*Porca miseria!* You think that you can make me believe that you didn't sleep with your fiancé?'

'I don't really care what you believe...'

'Then what kind of nonsense is this? I have never been promiscuous...why the hell are you looking at me like that?' he demanded in fierce condemnation.

Milly returned to her digging, thinking with inescapable bitterness and pain of the speed with which he had turned to another woman three years earlier. 'You shouldn't need to be told.'

The tense silence thundered and shouted and snarled. Flailed by pain and anger, Milly hacked at winter-bare brambles. 'I have cause to know that you're not always *careful* with—'

'I have never taken risks like that with anybody but you!' Gianni shot back in a savage undertone.

'Then why with me?' Milly glanced up enquiringly.

His lean brown hands closed into powerful fists. He swung restively away from her. 'That was different...'

'How was it different?'

He didn't answer her. 'A clean bill of health,' he ground out instead, as if he was spitting tacks, apparently choosing to settle for the lesser of two evils. 'OK. I already have that. My most recent medical was less than a month ago.'

But if Gianni thought he was getting off the hook that easily he was mistaken. Milly wasn't finished yet. 'I will also expect total fidelity.'

His eyes shot like flaming golden arrows into hers, his incredulity unfeigned. '*Accidenti*...where do you get the nerve to demand that of *me*?'

'I'm thinking of Connor's need for stability.' Cheeks

burning, because her own needs had risen first and foremost to her mind, Milly focused on the distant wall.

'*Connor?*' Gianni repeated rawly.

'You must set Connor a good example. Our son must be able to respect our marriage. So you can't have a mistress,' Milly informed him, warming to her theme by the second. 'And if I were to discover that you had been unfaithful, I'm afraid I would have to divorce you. I won't have Connor damaged by a destructive relationship.'

All tight-mouthed tolerance now fully breached, Gianni slashed a savage hand through the air. 'You are lecturing me about...*fidelity?*' His Sicilian accent was so thick she had to strain to comprehend that final word.

'I don't think it's a *lecture* to state what I want up front,' Milly responded stubbornly. 'And, after all, you *did* say that you had put the past behind you...'

Sheer rage turned Gianni pale beneath his vibrant bronze skin. In seething silence he studied her, as if he just could not believe that she had dared to remind him of that statement.

'And finally,' Milly added not quite steadily, watching the ice front settle over him like her most dangerous old enemy, 'I'm not prepared to sign a pre-nuptial contract.'

At that provocative announcement Gianni appraised her with eyes that would have chilled a polar bear, aggression emanating from every dangerously still and silent inch of him.

'Not because I have any desire to get my hands on a larger share of your wealth,' Milly explained heavily. 'But because I believe that the absence of a pre-nuptial contract will make it easier for you to respect our marriage. You see, you don't respect me, but I think you *will* respect what a divorce might cost you.'

Gianni stared at her with cold, brooding menace.

Milly shook her head in a sudden helpless gesture of despair. 'Gianni...when I left Paris, I also left everything you ever gave me behind. The clothes, the jewellery, the credit cards. I took nothing. Doesn't that at least prove that I'm not the mercenary type?' Her own voice emerged with a quality of pleading that embarrassed her, and hurriedly she compressed her lips.

Eyes black and reflective as mirrors, Gianni simply swung on his heel and started to walk away.

Milly suppressed a groan.

'Gianni!' she called.

He didn't even pause.

She hurried after him and then forced herself to a halt, watching in frustration as he receded from her with every impossibly long stride. 'Gianni, if you agree to my conditions...I'll try really hard to make everything the way it was!'

Abruptly he stopped dead, but he didn't turn round.

'It's going to be very difficult, but I'll *try* to learn to trust you again,' Milly completed huskily, tears thickening her throat as she thought of what they had once had and had so brutally had taken from them.

Gianni swung back. He sent her a scorching look of rampant disbelief. *You* will try to trust *me* again? Speech wasn't necessary. A split second later, he turned his arrogant dark head away and strode through the crumbling gateway out of sight.

Well, you handled him like a real pro, didn't you? Never had Milly seen a satisfied smile die faster. And her own emotions were all over the place. Until Gianni had appeared, she honestly hadn't appreciated the depth of her own bitterness. But three years ago Gianni had hurt her *so* much. In a blaze of publicity, he had taken off to the Caribbean with a supermodel, infinitely more beautiful than Milly could ever be. And Milly had immediately to her house in Paris, and had sat waiting, torn apart but struggling to understand what he was going through, and still hoping against hope that their unborn child would eventually bring Gianni back within talking distance, even if it only meant he lifted the phone.

With deeply troubled eyes, she watched the helicopter

take off again as she walked back towards the house. She hadn't meant for that to happen. She hadn't meant to drive him away again. Connor would be upset. Oh, for heaven's sake, why didn't she just admit it? *She* was upset!

The following morning Milly's portable phone, switched on since Gianni's departure, buzzed at seven. She had just got out of the bath. She leapt for the phone.

'You drive a hard bargain,' Gianni murmured softly. 'But so do I...'

Sinking down on the carpet, huddled in a towel, Milly nodded without speaking, tension strangling her ability to respond.

'You promise me that the past stays buried—'

'I *can't* do that!'

'And you don't ever tell me you love me again.'

Milly gritted her teeth and bowed her head over her knees. Gianni loosed a cynical laugh. 'I thought you'd be able to manage that one...'

'I'm damned if I do...and I'm damned if I don't, aren't I?' Milly countered painfully.

'Only a week ago you were madly in love with another man—'

'And then I got my memory back and *everything* changed!' Milly argued vehemently. 'Judging me on that isn't fair... I—'

She snapped her mouth shut in despair, for she knew now that she had never loved Edward. She had wanted to love him and had convinced herself that she did. The illusion had vanished the instant she got her memory back. But even before that point she had been responding to Gianni. Dear heaven, she had gone to bed with him again! Was it any wonder that he saw that wanton surrender as yet more evidence that her emotions ran only skin-deep?

'Gianni...think what you want,' Milly sighed.

'I always do. I also want to celebrate my way,' he murmured silkily. 'I'll need you tonight at the house in Paris—'

She stiffened in astonishment. 'You still *have* the house?'

Aware that Gianni had only bought that house for her occupation, and equally aware of the ruthless efficiency with which he usually cut loose from the past, she was genuinely amazed that he hadn't long since sold it.

'Around seven,' Gianni continued, as if she hadn't spoken. 'You'll be picked up this afternoon and you'll be back with Connor early tomorrow.'

'But I don't have a passport!' Milly was wildly disconcerted by his proposition. 'I lost it three years ago and I never applied for one as Faith Jennings, so if you're thinking that I—'

'You didn't *lose* your passport, *cara*. You left it behind in the townhouse and I eventually took it back to London with me. Fortunately it's still current, and it'll be waiting for you to collect at the airport. How did you contrive to get back into the UK without it?' Gianni enquired drily.

'I was a ferry passenger. I didn't realise I didn't have my passport until just before I got off. I was ready to panic, but in the end I wasn't actually challenged,' Milly recalled ruefully. 'In the crush I managed to slip through. But I've never been so nervous in my life and it's not something I'd ever try again. I felt like a criminal, waiting for a hand to fall on my shoulder.'

'I wish Immigration had picked you up and thrown you in a cell until I caught up with you,' Gianni confided grimly. 'I wasted a lot of time searching France for you!'

'I don't want to come to Paris tonight,' Milly admitted in a taut undertone.

'It's not negotiable. I'll see you later,' Gianni countered, and finished the call.

Celebrating *his* way? In Paris, where they had been happiest? Stefano had never set foot in the townhouse. The moment Gianni's brother came into her mind Milly tried to push him out again, but her bitterness rose simultaneously and it was impossible to evade her memories...

Gianni had kept Milly and Stefano in separate compartments. If Stefano hadn't chosen to breach those boundaries, Milly believed she would never have met him. Throughout their entire relationship Gianni had maintained his own homes in New York and London, and although he had occasionally mentioned Stefano, he had never once suggested that they should meet.

Stefano was Gianni's half-brother, born of his putative father's relationship with his stepmother. At the age of eleven, Stefano had been taken to Sicily and Gianni had become his legal guardian. Milly had first met Stefano at the New York apartment which Gianni had purchased for her use. By then Stefano had been studying at Harvard. He had just arrived on the doorstep one evening when Gianni was staying.

'I hardly see Gianni any more. Now I now why!' Stefano had laughed.

Initially, Gianni had been uneasy about his kid brother's descent, but, knowing how fond he was of Stefano, Milly had been pleased. It was so hard now to remember that she herself had once liked Stefano.

He had been immature, and pretty spoilt by Gianni's indulgence, but he had been easy company. During the final months of her relationship with Gianni, Stefano had called in whenever she was over in New York. Sometimes Gianni had been there; sometimes he hadn't been. Registering that Gianni had actually been enjoying the fact that he was seeing more of his brother, Milly had made every effort to be welcoming.

'If my brother really cares about you, he should marry you,' Stefano had said once, seriously embarrassing her.

But at the time she'd thought little of that comment— certainly hadn't registered that Stefano's interest in her had become rather too personal. After all, Stefano had had a live-in girlfriend of his own. And Milly had been very wrapped up in Gianni and her own concerns. It had been shortly after first meeting Stefano that she had discovered that she was pregnant.

Even after Gianni had told her that he didn't want to lose her, Milly had gone on feeling insecure. He hadn't ever said up front that he wanted their baby. And although he had been more tender and caring in all sorts of quiet ways she had feared that he was simply making the best of a bad situation. She had also waited for Gianni to tell his brother that she was pregnant. When Gianni had stayed silent, Milly had become more and more uneasy about his attitude.

The night that her world had fallen apart, she had been alone when Stefano dropped in to visit. He had been drinking, and for the first time Milly had felt uncomfortable with him, although even at that late stage she hadn't understood why—until he'd spoken, and shattered the casual camaraderie she had believed they'd had.

'You just don't see me, do you?' Stefano launched at her bitterly, his darkly handsome features flushed as the condemnation simply erupted from him. 'I don't exist for you except as Gianni's brother. I come round here to see you and all we ever talk about is *him.*'

'I don't understand…what—?'

'I'm in love with you!' Stefano shot at her accusingly. 'You haven't even noticed, have you?'

Milly was aghast, exploded out of her self-absorption with a vengeance. 'You've had too much to drink…you don't know what you're saying—'

'Don't talk down to me like I'm some little kid!' Stefano rounded on her furiously. 'You're not much older than I am. But Gianni's *years* older. He's almost a different generation! You've got much more in common with me—'

'Let's just forget you ever said this stuff,' Milly cut in tautly. 'You have to know how I feel about your brother—'

'And how does he *feel* about you?' Stefano slammed back, the words slurring. 'He jets in, takes you to bed and jets off again. All he does is *use* you…can't you see that?'

'I won't discuss our relationship with you,' Milly said shakily, seriously stung by that assessment.

'Don't tell me I leave you stone-cold. I won't believe you.

I've never met a girl who didn't think *I* was something special!' Stefano launched at her like a spoilt little boy, needing to blow his own trumpet. 'I'd treat you like a queen, Angel.'

'I've had enough of this, Stefano. I've only ever thought of you as Gianni's brother and I'm going to forget this ever happened, just like you'll want to forget it tomorrow morning,' Milly forecast witheringly. 'Now I'm going to call a taxi so that you can go home.'

'I'll call my own cab when I'm ready to leave,' Stefano informed her truculently. 'This is Gianni's place, not yours. I've got every right to be here if I want to be!'

While he angrily paced the room, his clumsy gait telling her that he was a lot drunker than she had initially appreciated, a wave of sick dizziness ran over Milly. But the look of utter misery in Stefano's brown eyes still hit her hard, making her feel responsible, even though she was well aware that she had never done or said anything which might have encouraged him. 'Look, it's just a crush, Stefano. That's all it is—'

'It's not a crush! I really, *really* love you!'

Nausea stirred in her stomach. 'But I'm not attracted to you—'

'You could be if you'd let yourself,' Stefano had flung stubbornly. 'I may not be the stud Gianni is, but I'm no teenage virgin!'

Milly's nausea grew suddenly worse. 'Look, let yourself out. I'm not feeling well. I'm going to bed!' she gasped as she raced like a maniac for the privacy of the bathroom that adjoined her bedroom.

She was horribly sick. As she slowly recovered from that bout, she heard what she assumed to be the slam of the front door on Stefano's departure. She meant to go and do up the locks and switch out the lights, but she ended up going for a shower instead. She was exhausted, and very upset. And her distress was exacerbated by the conviction that she would have to keep the whole messy episode a secret from Gianni.

How could she confide in him without causing friction between the two brothers? She didn't want to be the source of the smallest conflict between Gianni and his only living relative. And, although she didn't acknowledge it at the time, she was also afraid to add any further stress to their own relationship.

So, although Milly desperately longed to reach for the phone to talk to Gianni about what had happened, she resisted the temptation and staunchly told herself that it would all blow over. Stefano had got drunk to make that foolish declaration. When he sobered up, he would be angry that he had made a fool of himself. He would stay away from her from now on.

She pulled on a nightdress and climbed into bed. The bedroom door was still ajar. The light in the corridor was still on. Too weary even to get out of bed to turn it off, she stuffed her face in a pillow and went to sleep. It didn't once cross her mind that she might *not* be alone in the apartment...

With an angry shiver, Milly sank back to the present. She still found it so hard to credit that the reckless, selfish arrogance of a teenager unable to tolerate rejection could have devastated her life.

CHAPTER NINE

As THE limo which had picked Milly up at Charles de Gaulle airport wafted her through Paris that evening, her every thought was a memory...

Gianni had bought her the finest chocolates, perfume, and taken her to dine at exclusive restaurants. His knowledge of Paris related only to the exclusive haunts of the rich. Milly had returned the favour by making him queue up for ice-cream from her favourite parlour, browse for books, wander through the flea markets, enjoy the jazz festival and watch French plays in the Shakespeare garden in the Bois de Boulogne.

Employing the keys which had been waiting with her passport for her to collect, Milly let herself into the town-house on the Rue de Varenne. As she discarded her coat, her heart was beating very fast. She scolded herself for her nervous tension. Everything would be different. Since Gianni had retained the house for his own use, he would have made sweeping changes. The vibrant colours, exotic throws and comfortable furniture she had favoured would have been superceded by classic shades, cool elegance and superb antiques.

So it was a real shock for Milly to walk into the spacious reception rooms and see everything exactly as she had left it three years earlier. Her steps quickened as she took a tour and finally hurried upstairs to the bedroom they had once shared. The connecting door stood wide on the fabulous marble bathroom.

Milly focused on the giant bath, her breath catching in her throat as she remembered the night she had bathed in bubbles and Gianni had stolen that photograph. Racing after him, clutching a towel, she had cornered him in the bedroom.

'Give me that camera!' she had yelled furiously.

'Come and get it,' Gianni had invited, stunning dark eyes brimming with vibrant amusement as she had dripped all over the carpet.

'*Gianni*...I'm warning you!'

As he had stood there, naked but for a pair of silk boxer shorts, his lithe, bronzed body a powerful enticement, a wolfish grin had slashed his mouth and sent her treacherous pulses racing. '*Dio mio*, you're so sexy when you get aggressive.'

Milly had made a wild grab for the camera, but Gianni had cast it aside and caught her up in his arms to crush her mouth with hungry urgency under his.

'I want that film destroyed,' she had told him breathlessly, a long while later, still trembling from the raw potency of his stormy possession.

Gianni had given her a slow-burning smile and had said nothing.

So intense was that recollection that Milly stared at the bed almost as if she expected to see the ghosts of Gianni and herself *still* lying there. She blinked, and turned around in an uncoordinated circle, and then found herself heading for the fitted units in the dressing room. She stared in frank astonishment at the clothing carefully stored in garment bags and then sped into the bathroom to check cupboards.

Finally, with her legs threatening to buckle, she sank down on the corner of the bed. Unbelievable as it was to her, Gianni had left all her belongings intact. Nothing had been changed, nothing had been dumped. It was eerie. But for the garment bags, the past three years might not have happened. The whole house appeared to be locked in an astonishing time warp.

'You wouldn't believe how often I've pictured you here like this...' That deep, dark sexy drawl slashed through her reverie and sent her head flying up, shining waves of hair tumbling back from her oval face to accentuate troubled eyes as blue as lapis lazuli.

Milly looked fantastic, Gianni acknowledged with satisfaction, long past the stage of questioning why this one small woman should excite him to such an extent. It was sex, just sex. He was content with that explanation. It wasn't something he had to think about; the ache of hot, instantaneous arousal was reassuringly familiar. She was wearing something bright and clingy, which for Milly signified a fairly substantial degree of effort on her behalf. She was also trying to smile, but her eyes were strained. She was just nervous; she *had* to be happier than she looked, Gianni told himself impatiently, discarding that initial impression. He just could not see that she had the smallest thing to be unhappy about.

Milly stared at Gianni with colour steadily mounting in her cheeks. He lounged in the doorway, six feet three inches of stunning dark good looks and lean, lithe elegance, his attitude one of deceptive indolence.

Abruptly, she slid upright, smoothing uncertain hands down over the turquoise dress she wore. 'I didn't hear you arrive…'

Shimmering golden eyes roamed over her, lingering on the generous curve of her soft mouth, the defined thrust of her firm breasts and rounded hips in the sleek silky fabric. 'You've been shopping—'

'No. This was an impulse buy last year. I never wore it.'

'Sexy, *cara mia*,' Gianni told her with husky approval, slowly raising lean brown hands to shrug out of his overcoat and let it fall.

Milly's heart started to beat so fast she thought it might burst from her chest. He removed the jacket of the formal suit he wore beneath. Her breath began to rasp in her throat, making her mouth run dry. Without removing his smouldering attention from her for a second, he tugged loose his gold tie and unbuttoned his shirt.

'Gianni…' she began unevenly, her body reacting invol-

untarily to the wild, hot sexual charge in the atmosphere. As
her breasts swelled with languorous heaviness, and her nipples stiffened to push against the confines of her bra, she
shifted uneasily. 'We really should talk.'

'Never got us anywhere before.'

'Because we never actually *did* it!'

'Everything the way it was,' Gianni reminded her with
scorching golden eyes as he took an almost compulsive step
forward. 'You promised.'

Had she promised? Hadn't she just said she'd *try*? But as
Gianni came closer the question became academic as rational thought blurred and infinitely more basic promptings
took over. Suddenly she couldn't wait to get close. She
merged with his outrageously masculine frame on legs that
already felt weak and hollow, eagerly drawing in the familiar
warm, male scent of his skin.

'You want me...' Long fingers curved to her chin, exerting pressure to turn up her face and see the hunger she
couldn't hide.

Breathless, she gazed up into his spectacular eyes, heat
spearing up almost painfully in her stomach to stretch every
nerve-ending taut. 'Always.'

'That's all I need, *cara mia*,' Gianni asserted with complete conviction.

She reached up to him first, encouraging him to drive her
lips apart in a devouringly hungry kiss. Her head spun and
her senses whirled. He tasted like water in the desert, so
sweet, so precious she felt she would die if she didn't drink
deep. Painful memories fell away from her. She met those
dark, deep flashing eyes with an instinctive sense of coming
home.

Unzipping her dress, Gianni peeled it off. She shivered,
pressed her thighs together, seeking to contain the heat he
had already awakened. But in one easy movement she un-
clasped her own bra. Her face burned, but she revelled in
the sudden blaze of gold in Gianni's appreciative appraisal
as her pouting breasts fell free.

'Witch,' he rasped, tumbling her down backwards on the bed with a thrilling lack of cool.

Her spine curved in wondering pleasure as his expert mouth travelled hungrily between her urgently sensitive nipples. As he sucked on a straining pink bud she gasped, her hands clutching at shoulders still frustratingly sheathed in fabric.

'Take your clothes off,' she urged shakily.

Expelling his breath in a driven hiss, Gianni raised himself. He scrutinised her flushed face and moist parted lips with ravenous desire, his lean, strong features taut with the effort self-control demanded. Beginning to sit up, she arched her back, and his mesmerised gaze welded to the projecting peaks of her exquisite breasts.

'*Dio*... I can't spare that much time,' Gianni groaned raggedly.

He curved a not quite steady hand to her temptingly swollen flesh and then drove her flat again with the onslaught of his passionate mouth on hers. His tongue dipped with slow, skilful intimacy between her parted lips, tasting her with an eroticism that released a startled moan of excitement from her throat.

With a roughened laugh of satisfaction, Gianni lifted his head again and surveyed her. 'I might want to jump you like a starving animal, but tonight is going to be different,' he swore, rubbing a thumb gently along the ripe curve of her full lower lip, and she shivered with helpless anticipation.

'Different?'

'*Special,*' Gianni husked thickly against her mouth, and kissed her again. This time she didn't just see cymbals and fireworks, she saw a whole chamber orchestra illuminated by shooting rockets.

'I love the way you kiss,' she confided feverishly as she tried to wrench him out of his shirt. 'But if you don't take your clothes off I'll scream!'

Gianni finally backed off the bed. The slashing grin of

appreciation lightening his strong dark features squeezed her heart as efficiently as a vice.

Her softened eyes roamed over him. Not even the most perfectly tailored trousers could conceal the bold jut of his erection. A twist of almost shocking excitement slivered through her. Dry-mouthed, she watched him strip.

'I like it when you can't take your eyes off me,' Gianni confessed huskily.

Her whole body tingled with the need to touch him. He was awesomely aroused. He strolled fluidly back to the bed and she felt as if her bones were about to melt beneath her skin. He stood her up with gentle hands and went down on his knees to tug her panties down over her hips.

'I have three years of erotic daydreams to live out.' Gianni's deep, dark drawl fractured as he pressed his mouth in a surprisingly tender salute against her stomach. She quivered like a sapling in a storm.

Curving strong hands to her slender hips, he lifted her back on the bed. She was weak with hunger. His first touch was like a match hitting a bale of hay. She was so ready she already ached for him, but Gianni was intent on reacquainting himself with every responsive inch of her wildly sensitised flesh. With silken finesse, he explored the hot, moist centre of her. She writhed out of control. Then he rearranged her, like a gourmet at a feast, and used his wickedly expert mouth and tongue to drive her crazy with an intimacy that drove her from ecstatic moans to choked and frantic pleas for satisfaction.

'Dio…I love torturing you with pleasure…I've had nothing else on my mind since the day I saw you at the airport, cara mia. I can't work; I can't sleep,' Gianni ground out, startling her.

Rising over her, he settled her beneath him. He entered her with an evocative groan of shuddering satisfaction. She met his shimmering dark eyes, feeling the sheer burning intensity of his pleasure for a split second before he plunged her back into sole awareness of her own.

'You feel like hot satin!' Gianni rasped.

And then, as he moved on her and in her, the hot, electrifying excitement took over and she wrapped herself round him, moaning her pleasure beneath his every thrust. Heart and body exulting as one, she gave herself without inhibition and reached a shattering climax that left her floating in shell-shocked contentment.

Releasing her from his weight, Gianni hauled her back into the circle of his arms. The almost forgotten reassurance of that continuing desire for physical closeness even after satiation filled her with brimming warmth.

He ran a slow fingertip down over one tear-wet cheek. 'Special,' he breathed almost harshly, gazing intently into her drowningly blue eyes, dark colour slowly rising to accentuate his sculpted cheekbones. 'And yet you have driven me crazy more times than any woman I've ever known...'

'Really?' Milly gave him a dreamy, unapologetic smile.

'Really, *cara mia*,' Gianni confirmed, hungrily kissing her again.

Gianni woke up and rolled over. Milly wasn't there. He sat up with a jerk to hit the lights and check his watch. It was midnight. Springing out of bed stark naked, he strode out of the bedroom.

He found Milly downstairs in the dimly lit state-of-the art kitchen. Her slender back turned to him, she was barefoot and wearing an oversized T-shirt that he recognised as having once been his. Humming softly to herself, she was checking something in the stainless steel oven. The almost forgotten aroma of baking apples and pastry assailed Gianni. He turned pale.

Breathing in shallow, quiet spurts to refill his straining lungs, Gianni slowly unclenched his coiled fists. He was in a cold sweat! Swinging soundlessly out of the doorway, he flung himself back against the wall in the dark corridor beyond. Where *did* you think she'd gone? His even white teeth gritted. He was outraged by the recognition of his own fear, alienated by the dark, deep stirrings of childhood memories he always kept locked away.

When he'd been barely more than a toddler, Gianni had learnt the hard way that he couldn't depend on anybody. Not his mother, who had thrown him out of the house for hours on end while she entertained her clients, not his supposed father, who had drunk himself into violent rages and seized on any excuse to lash out with his fists and his belt. Not his stepmother, who had loathed him on sight and humiliated him at every opportunity.

Not even his deeply religious uncle and aunt, who had removed him from the orphanage at the age of thirteen and flown him over to their London home to take the place of their own dead son. For a little while he had believed he was really wanted, until they'd started constantly reminding him of the debt he owed them. They had never formally adopted him, and had washed their hands of him entirely the instant they were forced to accept that he had no vocation to become a priest.

Yet Milly's warmth and affection had drawn Gianni even as he'd marvelled at her naivety in being so foolishly, dangerously open. Didn't she know he was going to hurt her? Didn't she know he had nothing to give back? That deep down inside, where she was all giving and feeling, he was just one big, empty hollow? But fate had had the last and cruellest laugh on him. The day Gianni had found Milly with his brother had been the day he'd finally realised how much he loved her.

Levering himself off the cold wall with sudden force, Gianni went back upstairs and headed straight for the shower, wrenching on the controls with angry hands. Love had been a breeze for Milly. But love had been a killer-chiller for him. So she needn't think that sneaking out of bed in the middle of the night to make some childish offering of his once favourite snack was likely to change the status quo!

*   *   *

Milly carried the tray upstairs. She was so happy. She was just so incredibly happy. Gianni had been so tender, so teasing, so warm. It had honestly been as if the Stefano episode had never happened.

How Gianni could shut it all out, *how* he could be like that with her while still believing what he did, she could not begin to comprehend. But suddenly it didn't seem to matter. If that worked for him right now, that was all right with her. Only once they were safely married Gianni was in for a rather unpleasant surprise, she conceded ruefully. If it took her fifty years, if it took chaining him to a wall in a locked room, she would make him listen to her about Stefano!

Fully awake, Gianni was lounging in bed, intent on his notebook computer. His black hair was still damp from the shower he had evidently taken. His sleek, powerful bronzed body was dark and exotic against the pale bed linen. Milly studied him with wholly possessive eyes. Externally he was absolutely gorgeous, internally he was a little bit complicated, but they finally had a future and she intended to make the most of the opportunity.

'I thought you might be hungry…' She slid the tray down beside him, suddenly feeling self-conscious. Possibly it had been slightly over the top to rush down to the kitchen and turn out a *tarte tatin*.

'I'm not, but don't let me inhibit you,' Gianni murmured, without taking his eyes from the screen.

'It's something you like,' she told him.

Gianni glanced at the laden tray. Then he glanced up at her, brilliant dark eyes cool, questioning, filling her with instant discomfiture. 'I may not employ a chef here, but whatever I want I *can* afford to send out for,' he reminded her with sardonic softness. 'So why the hell did you feel the need to get out of bed at this hour to bake?'

Hot, mortified pink flooded Milly's cheeks. She snatched the tray back off the bed, but she wanted to pitch it at him.

'I don't require cute little domesticated gestures from you now,' Gianni added in measured addition.

The tray rattled in her tensing grasp. But for the two cups of hot coffee, she would definitely have dumped the lot on his lap. Shaken and angered by his volatile change of mood, Milly returned the tray to the kitchen. Why was Gianni behaving like this all of a sudden?

In bed, he had been so different. Dear heaven, why was she always so stupid around Gianni? *In bed*. Within those two simple words dwelt the explanation. The minute Gianni had satisfied that high-voltage sex drive of his, he just went right back to despising her again. Well, she refused to put up with that sort of treatment. She hadn't sunk that low yet. Or *had* she?

Hadn't she let Gianni fly her over for the night like a call-girl? A sure thing? She had definitely been a sure thing. Anguish infiltrated Milly at that acknowledgement. And hadn't she played a full and uninhibited part in her own downfall? Tonight she had been his puppet on a string...his totally abandoned puppet on a string. She squirmed, fingers curling on the stack of plates she had left lying out on the counter.

'Are you coming back to bed?' Gianni enquired with studied casualness from the doorway.

As Milly turned, her eyes lit on him like burning blue stars. She grabbed up a plate and hurled it with all her might. Looking genuinely startled, Gianni ducked. The plate smashed bare inches from him. She sent a second plate flying with similar accuracy. 'If I wanted to hit you, I *could*,' she told him furiously. 'So get out of here before I forget that violence is not an answer!'

Gianni straightened with admirable cool. 'OK...if it's that important, I'll eat it,' he breathed grittily.

Milly studied him with huge blue eyes and slowly shook her golden head. 'Why are you so stupid?' she whispered helplessly.

'Why are you?' Gianni responded, ice-cold.

Milly spun away, denying the cruel message in his diamond-hard eyes. He could make passionate love to her over and over again but he wouldn't allow her to harbour the smallest illusion about the precise nature of their relationship *out* of bed. Sentimental touches of the 'cute' and 'domesticated' variety were out of line. When he had said he wanted everything the way it had once been between them, he had really been lying in his beautiful white teeth. All he really wanted was all the sex he could handle.

'If I hurt your feelings, I'm sorry, but we need to start out straight,' Gianni murmured flatly.

He'd done it deliberately. She knew he had rejected her stupid edible offering deliberately. But she also knew she didn't want to force a major confrontation *before* they got married. Was that proof of her intelligence or proof of her cowardice?

Feeling wretched, she cleaned up the broken plates and then went back upstairs to the bedroom. A small jeweller's box with a very impressive logo awaited her on her pillow. She lifted the tiny box and set it unopened on the cabinet.

Sliding into bed, she was careful not to even glance at Gianni, and she turned her back on him. She had let him see how much he had hurt her and that stung her pride.

'It's a ring,' Gianni advanced, without any expression at all.

Grudging curiosity stirred Milly, because he had never given her a ring before. Reclaiming the box, she flipped it open on a spectacular ruby surrounded by diamonds.

She threaded the ring onto her right hand and said, with all the enthusiasm of a woman confronting a huge pile of dirty washing, 'Fantastic. Thanks.'

'You're wearing it on the wrong finger,' Gianni informed her drily.

Milly frowned. 'Sorry?'

'It's an engagement ring,' Gianni extended in a charged undertone.

Milly flipped right over to look at him, blue eyes rounded with incredulity. 'An *engagement* ring?'

'Why not? We're getting married.' His bold profile rigid, Gianni doused the lights.

End of discussion. In the darkness, Milly fingered her engagement ring with rather more interest than she had been prepared to show a minute earlier. A romantic gesture? She reddened. Hardly. A conventional one? Gianni had yet to mention *when* they would marry. Milly tensed at that belated realisation. Was it possible that this was going to be a *very* long engagement? The sort of engagement that went on year after endless year until it became a positive joke to all onlookers?

'Hi...' Her expressive face pale and stiff, Milly slid behind the table in the dining room. An unfamiliar maid had wakened her.

'I'd have let you sleep, but I know you want to be back for Connor.' With a slow-burning smile that reminded Milly of how very lacking in restraint she had been around dawn, Gianni poured her a cup of coffee. 'You still look pretty tired.'

Milly reddened like an awkward teenager. While she had still been deliciously drowsy and defenceless Gianni had invaded her side of the bed, ruthlessly set on conquest. And even with all her experience of Gianni's incredible expertise she had been quite unprepared either for that level of slow, exquisite seduction or the intensity of his determination to give her the ultimate in pleasure. The intimate ache of her body had powered that smile he now felt able to bestow upon her.

She looked so miserable, Gianni reflected in frustration. He focused on her hand, where it rested on the table only about nine inches from his own. But Gianni was still challenged. Breathing in deep, he reached out suddenly to cover her tense fingers with his hand.

Milly froze in complete disconcertion. Gianni was not given to demonstrative gestures beyond the bedroom door.

She stared at him. His ridiculously lush black lashes semi-veiled his eyes, but his tension was pronounced.

'Last night, nothing went according to plan,' Gianni advanced, with the taut stiffness of a male who never normally allowed himself to explain anything he did. 'We had a reservation at Castel's. We were supposed to dine out. But coming back here, seeing you here again…'

As his hesitation threatened to stretch into a stark silence, Milly instinctively closed her other hand round his as well, literally holding him prisoner. 'Yes?' she encouraged in a breathless whisper.

'It was like we'd never been apart,' Gianni completed flatly.

'I thought that was what you wanted,' Milly muttered unevenly.

Gianni's strong jawline clenched. 'I did…I *do*…but for a while last night I didn't…'

Milly waited with bated breath, but the silence lingered. She was stunned by the extraordinary fact that Gianni had made the effort to explain that his passion had been entirely spontaneous and that he had originally planned a very different evening. Dinner and dancing at the most exclusive nightclub in Paris put the presentation of an engagement ring into a new light.

But his second admission had shaken her most of all. That had been Gianni telling her in as few words as possible that last night their unresolved past had returned to haunt him and caused his change of mood. It was such a gigantic step forward in communication that Milly's eyes glowed as if he had lit a neon light inside her. 'Gianni, I'm so pleased you told me this. I know how difficult—'

'And now that we've got that out of the way, *cara mia*,' Gianni interposed at speed, his lean, dark features lightening with barely concealed relief, 'We should talk about the wedding arrangements. I've applied for a special licence. We can get married this week.'

As a distraction, that change of subject worked. Having

been on the very brink of an emotional speech, Milly was stopped dead in her tracks. *'This week?'*

'Why not?' Gianni elevated a winged ebony brow. 'We have no good reason to wait.'

'I guess not…' Her attention welded to his spectacular dark eyes, Milly's response was rather weak. She had been so totally wrong in her suspicions. Gianni hadn't been using an engagement ring as a delaying tactic. If anything, he was prepared to *rush* her to the altar.

'Connor needs me around,' Gianni pointed out.

Her dreamy smile faded. 'Yes, of course he does.'

Louise Barclay watched Milly twirl in her wedding dress. Reminiscent of a romantic Edwardian tea gown, it was an incredibly elegant confection of silk adorned with exquisite handmade lace which enhanced her slender figure.

'You really, *really* love this guy, don't you?' Louise breathed with a slightly dazed expression on her freckled face.

Milly fell still in apparent dismay at that charge. 'How do you know that?'

Louise assumed a mock air of deep concentration. 'Oh, it might be the way Gianni's name enters just about every sentence. Then again, it might be the totally off-this-planet look you have when you say his name—'

'Louise!' Milly groaned.

'Or it could even be the fact that you've phoned him four times in the last two hours. I've heard of bridal nerves, but the last two times you called he was downstairs under this very same roof,' Louise pointed out gently.

Milly went pink. 'Phone calls are like a jokey thing between us.'

'Hey, I'm not criticising. Obviously he's crazy about you too.'

Eyes clouding, Milly turned away. She hadn't actually seen Gianni for four days. Business had kept him abroad. But, since her return from Paris, Gianni had made regular calls, and on the phone he was Gianni as she remembered him. Tender, teasing and warm. That was why the phone had become her lifeline.

Louise sighed. 'Why didn't Gianni just organise a media man-hunt when you went missing three years ago?'

Milly stiffened. 'Strictly speaking, I wasn't missing. I left Paris because we'd split up. We had some major problems.'

Her friend grinned. 'But nothing the two of you couldn't surmount within a week of finding each other again!'

But Milly knew better. The Stefano episode would never be forgotten. She was certain that her supposed betrayal had come back to haunt Gianni that night in Paris, and it would keep on coming back until she dealt with it. But how *was* she to clear her own name?

What, after all, had changed? It would still be her word against Stefano's. Stefano would never tell the truth; he had too much to lose. But for all that, Milly mused, Stefano would surely be very shocked to learn that she was back in Gianni's life in the infinitely more secure role of his wife.

Her portable phone buzzed. She snatched it up. 'Gianni…?'

'I'm now on my way to the church. We haven't yet met any roadblocks or fallen trees—'

'Don't be snide.'

'Of course, some gorgeous flame from my past could still throw herself across the church steps and prevent me from reaching the altar—'

'That's not funny!' Milly cut in hotly.

'Milly…proceed to the bedroom door. That's the large wooden oblong with the handle. Open the door, walk down the stairs and get into the transport waiting,' Gianni instructed with gentle satire. 'If you keep me hanging around at that church, I'll—'

'You'll what?' Milly whispered in breathless interruption as she moved towards the door.

'You'll find out tonight,' he promised, in a roughened

sexy undertone that made her heartbeat accelerate at the most astonishing rate.

'I'm going to be awfully late, Gianni...'

'I won't wait.'

'You will,' she muttered, smiling, and finished the call.

On her way down the stairs, she was amazed by the number of staff bustling in and out of the ballroom, and she was about to ask what was happening when Robin Jennings strolled out of the drawing room to extend his arm to her with a broad grin.

'Gianni wanted me to surprise you.'

Milly gave the older man a delighted smile and a welcoming hug. 'I'm so glad you're here to share this day with me.'

After that first surprise, the surprises simply got larger. The church car park and the road outside were packed with luxury cars. As Robin helped her out of the limo Gianni's security men surged forward to shield her from a pack of eager photographers and journalists shouting questions.

'What's going on?' Milly voiced her bewilderment in the church porch.

'Gianni did mention that he wanted to show you off to the whole world,' Robin Jennings confided then. 'Only I didn't realise he meant it so literally.'

There wasn't even standing room left in the church.

Gianni watched Milly walk down the aisle with glittering dark eyes of appreciation.

The simple ceremony filled her with emotion and optimism. Some day soon, she swore, she would be able to tell Gianni how much she loved him without him acting as if it was verbal abuse of the most offensive kind.

'Why didn't you tell me you were inviting all these people?' Milly squealed, the minute she got him on his own in the limo. 'We'll be in all the newspapers tomorrow, and you know how you hate that sort of stuff! Everything that's happened to me will come out as well.'

Gianni's dark, deep flashing eyes shimmered with amusement. 'In the words of one of my PR team...''just like a fairytale''. Less than cool, but romantic. You're a living cross between the Sleeping Beauty and Cinderella. I'm still working on being a prince.'

'Did you really say you wanted to show me off to the whole world?'

Slight colour burnished his stunning cheekbones. 'I don't remember.'

Plunged into a reception for five hundred guests back at Heywood House, Milly found her wedding day an increasingly breathless whirl.

Around three that afternoon she slid away to speak privately to Davina Jennings. After the older woman had listened to Connor's excited chatter and cuddled him, she explained that Edward had now become a junior partner in Jennings Engineering.

'He's bearing up very well to having lost you, I have to admit,' Davina confided ruefully. 'With hindsight, I can see that Edward *was* rather more interested in the partnership than he was in you. You made the right decision.'

Davina pressed a very familiar item of jewellery into Milly's hand. 'The bracelet. You left it behind in your room.'

'But I can't keep it. It belonged to your grandmother,' Milly protested.

'You're always going to be part of our family, Milly,' the older woman told her gently. 'But now that you've got your memory back, I'd love to know how you acquired the bracelet in the first place.'

'A couple of days before the accident, I bought it off a market stall.' Milly had turned the silver bracelet over and noticed the word 'Faith' inscribed on the back. It hadn't occurred to her that it might be a name. She had seen it in the light of a message to have faith, keep faith no matter how difficult things might seem. She had clasped it round her wrist like a talisman the same day she'd boarded the train to Cornwall.

'The bracelet belongs with you now. At least you liked it enough to buy it,' Davina remarked wryly. 'Enough of that. Have the police been in touch with you about the accident?'

'Gianni suggested that I get in touch with them, so I made a fresh statement the day before yesterday,' Milly admitted with a rueful twist of her lips. 'I'm afraid that even with my memory back I still didn't have any useful facts to offer them.'

'That can't be helped. By the way, Gianni mentioned the enquiries he's having made on our behalf. If our long-lost daughter *can* be traced, I've no doubt he's the man to do it. Yet that awful day he made us tell you the truth I didn't trust him an inch.' The older woman grimaced. 'I should've recognised that, having found you, he was simply *terrified* of losing you again!'

Milly laughed at that idea. 'Gianni has nerves of steel!'

'Not where you're concerned,' the older woman replied with quiet conviction.

After a light supper was served at seven, Connor fell asleep on Milly's lap. Gianni lifted his slumbering son gently from her. 'It's time he went to bed.'

Barbara Withers was dancing, and very much preoccupied with her partner. Gianni was ready to intervene, but Milly scolded him with reproachful eyes and gave him a little lecture on the need to consider the feelings and the needs of his employees.

'How many employees have you had?' Gianni enquired as he carried Connor upstairs.

'None...but I know what's right,' Milly retorted, not one whit deflated. 'And sometimes you're just a bit too bossy and demanding.'

Gianni met her look of fearless challenge and threw back his head to laugh. '*Dio mio*...how I have missed you in my life!'

At that admission, her breath caught in her throat. ''Sometimes I wonder if I lost my memory because I couldn't handle remembering the pain,' she confided shakily.

The sudden silence that fell seemed to hang on a knife-edge. Aware that she had breached forbidden barriers, Milly scooped Connor out of Gianni's arms and got on with putting him to bed. By the time she had finished their exhausted toddler was no longer fast asleep.

'Play cars?' he mumbled drowsily to Gianni.

Hoping to distract their son until he went off again, Milly picked up a toy car and ran it along the top of his duvet. 'I can give you ten minutes.'

'Boys play cars,' Connor muttered dismissively.

'I wonder where he picks up these sexist ideas,' Gianni remarked, with sudden vibrant amusement.

'It's the Sicilian blood, Gianni. It's in his genes,' Milly teased, highly relieved that the awkward moment had been successfully bridged.

But it wasn't to be the last awkward moment. A pretty brunette teenager hurried up to speak to Gianni when they returned to the ballroom. 'Why's Stefano not here?' she asked baldly.

Gianni's long fingers tensed on Milly's spine. 'He's not well.'

'Gosh, is it serious?'

'I shouldn't think so,' Gianni countered.

'Poor Stefano,' the girl groaned sympathetically. 'He never seems to have much luck these days, and yet he used to be so much fun.'

'Maybe he just grew up,' Gianni suggested flatly.

He whirled Milly fluidly away onto the dance floor. It was some minutes before she could breath normally again, and even longer before she felt the worst of the tension ease in Gianni's big powerful frame. *Had* he invited Stefano to their wedding? Or had she just heard a social excuse to cover the absence of his one and only brother?

'I wanted this to be a wonderful day,' Gianni breathed harshly.

'It *has* been,' Milly argued. 'Don't you ever dare think otherwise! I've met hundreds of people, who have all been incredibly nice to me. I've got to be the centre of attention without anybody thinking I was a show-off! And for the first time in our entire relationship you have switched off your mobile phone!'

His dark, deep flashing eyes roamed over her animated face with an intensity that made her heart sing. Easing her closer, he complained about the frustrating difference in their heights and then, with a growl of very male impatience, he just lifted her high off her startled feet. He kissed her with such desperately hungry need she was trembling when he finally lowered her back to solid earth again.

'I need to be alone with you. I want you all to myself, *cara mia*,' Gianni growled in the circle of her arms.

'Well, you're just going to have to wait.'

'If we'd been able to take a honeymoon, we could have been out of here hours ago!' Gianni ground out in frustration.

'Why weren't we able?'

'Because we couldn't have taken Connor abroad with us. He has no documentation right now—'

Milly frowned. 'What do you mean?'

Gianni sighed. 'Milly, you slipped right back into your true identity because it was already established. Our son, however, was registered at birth as the child of Faith Jennings. That has to be legally sorted out before he can be issued with a new birth certificate.'

'My goodness, I never even thought about that!'

'It's in hand. Don't worry about it. But as soon as Christmas is over I have every intention of finding a hot, deserted beach and bringing in the New Year—'

'With Connor and a bucket and spade?'

'I'm not listening. Fantasy is all I've got right now,' Gianni muttered raggedly, whisking her deftly behind one of the marble pillars that edged the dance floor and hauling her up to his level again to repossess her soft mouth with hot, driven urgency.

Milly caught fire. 'Gianni—'

'You're like too much champagne in my blood.' He bowed his arrogant dark head over hers and snatched in a fracturing breath. 'You push me to the edge. Sometimes I need you so much it *hurts*.'

Already dizzy with desire, Milly experienced a joyous flare of sheer happiness. Had he noticed what he had said? Not want but *need*. Gianni, who prided himself on never needing anybody or anything, whose belief in self-sufficiency was legendary, had admitted that he needed her.

And yet a few hours later, when they were finally in the privacy of their own bedroom, surprisingly Gianni was patience personified. He removed her wedding dress with gentle, almost regretful hands. He told her how gorgeous she had looked all day. He made sweet, tender love to every sensitised, shivering inch of her he uncovered. He took his time—oh, yes, he took his time—until she was twisting and begging, lost in incoherent urgency. And when he at last sealed his lean, bronzed body to hers, and possessed her with aching sensuality, it was the most sensational experience they had ever shared.

Two weeks later, Gianni watched Milly turn on the lights on the big Christmas tree she had sited in the drawing room of Heywood House.

She smiled like a happy child when the lights worked first time. But then she'd had plenty of practice, Gianni conceded. This was the third tree she had dressed within as many days. Several shopping trips to Harrods and other well-known retail outlets had yielded a huge collection of ornaments and other necessities. It was a very big house, she had pointed out, in an apparent attempt to convince him that she was just doing what had to be done. But the truth was that Milly adored the festive season, gloried in every single tradition, no matter how naff, and still left out refreshment for Santa Claus as an adult.

'What do you think?' she prompted expectantly.

'Spectacular.' Gianni looked past the glimmering lights to

Milly, her fantastic hair tumbling round her shoulders, eyes bright as sapphires in her beautiful smiling face. 'Christmas just wasn't the same without you, *cara mia*.'

Milly stilled, veiling her eyes, not wanting to seem too conscious of that easy reference to the past. 'Wasn't it?'

'Like Scrooge, I stopped celebrating it,' Gianni admitted.

'Oh, Gianni!' Milly groaned, troubled by the imagery summoned up by that confession and heading towards him like a homing pigeon.

'And, like grumpy old Ebenezer, I took particular pleasure in doing it.'

Milly linked her arms tightly round his narrow waist. 'We're about to have the most wonderful Christmas ever!'

And it would be, Milly thought with warm confidence. They had spent every hour of the past two weeks together, loving and laughing. She had never been as happy as she was now. She had never known Gianni so relaxed or so content. She loved watching him with Connor, revelling in the rough-housing that little boys enjoy, but she loved him most of all for his acceptance of their son's occasional tantrums.

In fact, from that morning in Paris Gianni had been fantastic in every possible way. He had changed over their three years apart, she now acknowledged. He was more tolerant, more kind, less volatile, less driven. For Milly, it was deeply ironic that Gianni should be capable of showing her more caring tenderness now than he had shown her *before* he'd seen her wrestling on a bed with Stefano! And, unfortunately, that presented Milly with a major problem.

Every hour, on the hour, Gianni was proving that he could successfully put that sordid little scene behind him. As long as the subject was never broached, as long as it was left buried. She still couldn't really understand how he could contrive to achieve that miracle. Could it be because he knew that sexually nothing had really happened that night? Gianni had accepted his brother's lying explanation in its entirety. That *she* had been lonely and *he* had been drunk, that just for a few foolish minutes desire had overwhelmed decent boundaries.

Certainly Gianni had never doubted her guilt. She had been condemned for playing the temptress and punished much more heavily than Stefano. She was still very angry and bitter about that fact. But now she feared the risk she would be taking in challenging Gianni again. She might destroy everything they had recently regained; she might wreck their marriage.

And she still couldn't *prove* that she was innocent. To believe her, Gianni would have to accept that Stefano was an out-and-out liar, capable of behaviour that might well have landed him in court in any other circumstances. That was a very tall order. But, even as Milly confronted that truth, she knew that it wasn't possible for her to remain silent. She would just have to deal with the fall-out when it happened.

That same afternoon, Milly was coiled in Gianni's arms in front of the log fire in the library, telling him between kisses about the new rose garden she was planning, when a knock on the door interrupted them.

With a groan of annoyance, Gianni settled her into an armchair. Milly closed her eyes sleepily.

'Wake up, *cara mia*. We have a visitor.'

Something in Gianni's flat delivery spooked her. Her drowsy eyes opened very wide in dismay when she focused on the young man hovering in the centre of the magnificent rug. It was Stefano.

CHAPTER TEN

STEFANO had so much strain etched on his taut face he looked a lot older then he was. His hair was shorter now. He was a little too thin. His extrovert ebullience appeared to have deserted him. His dark eyes evaded both Milly's gaze and Gianni's.

Milly glanced at Gianni and just winced. The Sicilian side of Gianni's brooding temperament was in the ascendant. He looked grim as hell, but kind of satisfied too, content that his kid brother should be nervous as a cat in his radius. Milly began to revise her assumption that she had been punished more than Stefano. The two brothers had once been pretty close. Stefano, for all his brash talk and swagger, had been heavily dependent on Gianni's approval. And Gianni, she now recognised, had cut him loose from that support system.

Milly stood up. 'Anybody want a drink?' she gushed, to break the awful silence.

'No, thanks...I need to talk,' Stefano announced tautly.

'We'll talk elsewhere,' Gianni drawled, smooth as glass, but he shot Milly a grim, assessing glance, evidently having expected her to be more discomfited by Stefano's presence.

'I don't keep a hair shirt in my wardrobe,' Milly told Gianni defiantly.

'Milly has to be here,' Stefano stated stiffly. 'And you have to promise to hear me out, Gianni. I don't care what you do afterwards, but you've got to give me the chance to explain things.'

'Is there some point to that curious proviso?' Gianni enquired very drily.

Stefano lowered his head. 'You're my brother and I've wronged you,' he breathed tightly. 'I've lied to you, de-

167

ceived you, and I stood by and did nothing when I could have helped you. I followed the tabloid coverage after you got married. I found out what had happened to Milly...the hit-and-run and everything since...and I guess I just couldn't live with myself any more.'

Milly sank back down into her chair because her knees were wobbling. As far as the two men were concerned she might as well not have been there, and if the knowledge of their marriage had scared Stefano into confession mode, she had no desire to distract him.

Gianni was very still. '*How* have you lied?'

'About that night with Milly in New York,' his brother said gruffly.

'But you had no reason to lie. I saw the worst with my own eyes!' Gianni shot back at him.

'There's no way you'd ever have forgiven me for what I did!' Stefano burst out with sudden rawness. 'You'd have thought I was some sort of pervert. I *had* to lie! It was me or her, surely you can see that?'

Gianni was now the colour of ash beneath his bronzed skin, his hard facial bones fiercely prominent. 'Milly said you assaulted her...'

The silence hung like a giant sheet of glass, ready to crash.

Milly cleared her throat and spoke up. 'Stefano told me he loved me. He was drunk. I was feeling sick and I told him to go home,' she explained. 'I heard the front door slam while I was in the bathroom. I thought he'd left...'

'I opened the door and then I changed my mind,' the younger man mumbled.

'So I got into bed and went to sleep.'

Gianni scrutinised her taut face and then focused with mounting incredulity on his brother.

'I saw her sleeping. I just wanted to kiss her. That's all. I *swear*!' Stefano protested, weak as water now beneath the appalled look of menace and disgust flaring in Gianni's diamond-hard eyes.

'I think maybe you thought that if you kissed me, you'd be able to prove that I could respond to you,' Milly countered with contempt. 'You were angry with me. I'd dented your ego, and just for that you frightened the life out of me!'

'I was drunk as a skunk...I hardly knew what I was doing!'

Gianni's hands coiled into powerful punitive fists, and as he absorbed his kid brother's mute terror a look of very masculine revulsion crossed his lean, strong face. '*Accidenti*...I wonder how many sex offenders say that.'

Milly sprang upright again, her fine features flushed with turbulent emotion, and suddenly she was erupting like a volcano. '*You* needn't sound so blasted pious!' she fired bitterly at Gianni. 'If Stefano *had* been a rapist, you'd have given him open house. You just walked out and *left* me with him!'

Beneath the bite of that derisive attack Gianni froze, to stare back at Milly with stricken eyes.

Stefano's shoulders slumped as he too looked at Milly. 'I didn't mean to terrify you, but when you woke up you went crazy, like you were being attacked—'

'She *was* being attacked,' Gianni slotted in from between clenched teeth, his Sicilian accent thick as molasses as he visibly struggled to control his own rising fury. 'When you touch a woman without her consent, it's an assault.'

'I panicked! When you saw us, I was only trying to hold her still until she calmed down—'

'How the bloody hell do you expect me to believe that?' Gianni roared at the younger man in savage interruption. 'You are one sick bastard! *Per meraviglia*, you came to me that night in tears, sobbing out your penitence, telling me how you couldn't resist her, insinuating that she had led you on. It wasn't *enough* that you had assaulted a pregnant woman; you then chose to destroy our relationship to save your own useless hide!'

Stefano stumbled back against the desk for support. 'I didn't know she was pregnant then, Gianni. I'd never, ever have touched her if I'd known that! *Dio mio*...I pulled a crazy stunt and I frightened her, but I honestly didn't mean to!'

Milly studied the younger man with unconcealed scorn. 'I might be impressed by that defence if you'd thought better of your lies once you'd had time to appreciate what you'd done. But even weeks after that night in New York, you were still determined to keep on lying!'

Gianni's winged brows pleated. 'Are you saying that you saw Stefano *after* that night?' Gianni looked dazed.

'Gianni, once you asked me what I was doing in Cornwall three years ago. I'll tell you now. I went there to confront Stefano,' Milly stated crisply. 'I took a lot of trouble to find him. In the end I had to contact his girlfriend's mother and pretend to be a friend of hers to find out where they were staying.'

Stefano was now staring fixedly at the rug.

'You went to Cornwall to see him? *Why?*' Gianni's open bewilderment told her that shock had deprived him of his usual ability to add two and two.

'Milly wanted me to tell you the truth.' Stefano spoke up again in a sudden rush. 'She tried to shame me into it by telling me that she was pregnant, but I already knew that by then because you'd told me. I was furious she had tracked me down. I didn't want anything to do with her in case you found out. You might've started doubting my story, maybe thinking that we'd been having an affair...'

'Per amor di Dio...' Gianni gazed with incredulous dark eyes at his trembling kid brother, and then he simply turned his back.

'When I arrived at the cottage, Stefano had been drowning his sorrows again,' Milly revealed ruefully. 'He'd had a row with his girlfriend and she'd taken their hire car and driven back to London to fly home, leaving him stranded.'

'It was too *late* to tell the truth! I was in too deep by then. There was nothing else to do but face it out!' Stefano protested weakly.

Gianni's dark, haunted eyes were fixed to Milly. 'Tell me

that the night you're referring to was *not* the same night that you were hit by that car!' he urged, almost pleadingly.

'It *was* that night.' Milly shrugged fatalistically. 'I'd gone to the cottage in a taxi and then let it go.'

As Gianni rounded on Stefano, the younger man backed away, looking sick as a dog. 'Until I read about the hit-and-run in the papers last week, I didn't *know* what had happened to Milly that night! How *could* I have known? She just walked out on me. For all I knew she had a car parked further up the road—'

'You didn't give a damn either way,' Milly condemned helplessly. 'In a twisted way, you had started to blame *me* for the mess you were in with Gianni!'

'I called a cab the next morning and flew back to New York,' Stefano continued woodenly, as if she hadn't spoken. 'I had no idea that Milly had been injured after leaving the cottage.'

'But within days you were well aware that I was frantically trying to find her.' Gianni's tone was one of savage disbelief. 'Yet not one word did you breathe! You could have told me you'd seen her in Cornwall but you didn't. I spent months searching France for her. By then she had been wrongly identified as another woman.'

'I knew nothing about any of that,' Stefano reiterated, perspiration beading his strained face. 'And if I'm here now, it's because I couldn't stand all this on my conscience any more.'

'No, you're here now because Milly's my wife,' Gianni delivered with chillingly soft exactitude. 'Because you assumed I might already know all this, and the idea of confessing all and throwing yourself on my mercy seemed like the only option you had left.'

'That's not how it was, Gianni.' Stefano had turned a ghastly colour.

'Your conscience got to you too late. You hurt Milly not once, but twice. You also cost me the first years of my son's life,' Gianni condemned with lethal menace. 'But what I can never, ever forgive is my *own* mistake, Stefano. I put family loyalty first. And here you are, our father all over again. Weak, dishonest, unscrupulous. It's a just reward for my stupidity, isn't it?'

Looking at Gianni, Stefano seemed to crumple entirely. 'I'm not like that. I'm not. I've changed a whole lot since then. I *had* to lie… I was so scared—'

Gianni said something cold in Italian.

Stefano was openly begging now. 'How was I supposed to admit the truth, knowing that you'd kill me? Do you think I didn't realise that *she* came first with you when I saw how you reacted at the apartment? It was her or me…you've *got* to see that!'

Milly did not feel sorry for Stefano, but she was squirming for him. His best quality had always been the depth of his attachment to Gianni. He had always been measuring himself up against Gianni. He had probably developed a crush on her for the same reason. But alcohol, arrogance and sheer stupidity had combined to tear Stefano's privileged little world apart. He *had* been terrified that night in New York after Gianni had walked out on them both, terrified that Gianni, who had been more father than brother to him, would disown him.

'Go home, Stefano,' Milly suggested wearily.

Gianni said nothing. It was as if Stefano had become invisible. His brother slung him one last pleading glance and then hurried out of the room.

A hollow laugh that startled Milly was wrenched from Gianni then. '*Porca miseria!* To think I was jealous of that pathetic little punk!'

'Jealous?' Milly parroted in astonishment. 'Of *Stefano*?'

Gianni half spread expressive brown hands and then clenched them tight into defensive fists, his strong profile rigid as steel. He swallowed hard. 'Yes. Long before that night I saw you together at the apartment, I was *very* jealous,' he bit out raggedly.

Milly was stunned by that revelation. 'I can't believe that... I mean, why on earth—?'

'You had a bond with him. You talked about things I was totally out of touch with... *house* music, clubs. You used the same street dialect, shared the same *in* jokes,' Gianni enumerated with harsh emphasis. 'You were the same generation. I introduced you to dinner dates, antiques and art galleries, and occasionally you were bored out of your skull and I knew it.'

Milly was savaged by that shattering outpouring of feelings she would never have dreamt Gianni could experience. Insecurity, vulnerability concerning the age-gap between them. 'You couldn't expect us to share every taste, every interest...'

'I didn't feel that way until Stefano came into the picture.'

'I thought you were pleased we got on so well.'

'Sure I was pleased.' Gianni's agreement was raw with self-contempt. 'I'd ring you from the other side of the world and in the background my kid brother would be cracking jokes and making you laugh. I was *eaten* with jealousy and there was nothing I could do about it.' He moved restively about the room like a trapped animal, forced to pace round a too small cage. 'But until that night I saw you with him I *knew* it was all in my own mind; I *knew* I was being unreasonable!'

Suddenly Milly was grasping why Gianni had been so quick to believe her capable of betraying him. Jealousy rigidly suppressed—a fertile and dangerous breeding ground for distrust and suspicion. Yet she had never suspected that Gianni was jealous. Once he had even told her that he was grateful she had Stefano for company. His ferocious pride had ensured he went to great lengths to conceal his own weakness.

'I was planning to surprise you that night. I was in a really good mood. But I went haywire when I saw you on our bed with Stefano. That was my every worst fear come true. If I had stayed one second longer I would've torn him apart with my bare hands!' Gianni asserted in a smouldering undertone, ashen pale. 'I couldn't stand to even look at you. So I didn't.'

So I didn't. He always protected himself from what he didn't want to deal with emotionally.

'As usual, you took the easy out,' Milly sighed with immense regret.

The sudden silence seemed to swell.

'It wasn't the easy way out, *cara mia*,' Gianni contradicted from between bloodlessly compressed lips, feverish colour scoring his stunning cheekbones.

Milly hardened herself to the distinct shock spreading in the dark, deep flashing eyes pinned to hers. Now that the truth had come out, she wasn't prepared to allow him to duck that issue. 'Gianni, most men would've confronted us there and then. It's all right saying that you might have ripped Stefano apart. Frankly, I couldn't have cared less what you did to him that night! No, it was what you did *afterwards* that destroyed us.'

Gianni's breathing pattern fractured audibly. 'His *lies* destroyed us.'

'No. Your refusal to see me again did that,' Milly countered painfully, her blue eyes saddened. 'And I'm not interested in what you *thought* I'd done. I'd been with you for two years and I was carrying your child. I had the right to expect a meeting with you. But what did you do? You wouldn't even take a call from me and then you took off to the Caribbean with another woman!'

Gianni latched on to that last condemnation with something very much like relief. '*Accidenti*, you don't need to worry about that!' he assured her. 'We never actually made it between the same sheets. When it came down to it, I wasn't interested.'

'That's not the point,' Milly groaned, refused to be sidetracked into betraying the pleasure she'd received from that information. 'The point is that you let me down by refusing to face up to the situation between us.'

'Let me get this straight, *cara mia*,' Gianni breathed raggedly, as if she had suddenly discharged a shotgun into his back, brilliant eyes burning in stark golden disbelief. 'You're accusing me...Gianni D'Angelo...of running away like a spineless little jerk!'

Milly winced.

'Only you were trying to wrap it up a bit!' Gianni grated, outraged by her silence.

'Why did you take so long to tell Stefano that I was pregnant?'

Disconcerted, Gianni frowned. 'It was private, no business of his.'

'He's your brother.'

'When I hadn't yet decided how I intended to resolve the situation, I wasn't prepared to discuss it with anybody but you,' Gianni framed impressively.

'And not even with me if you could help it,' Milly tacked on helplessly. 'You spent that time trying to decide whether to keep me or dump me, didn't you?'

Gianni glowered at her. '*Dio*...it wasn't like that at all!'

'The speed with which you grabbed the first excuse you had to ditch me isn't in your favour,' Milly informed him.

'At the time, I was thinking of marrying you!'

'*Thinking?*' Milly repeated, unimpressed. 'Only it never got further than that. I trusted you. I relied on you. I loved you for two years and yet it still wasn't enough to convince you that we had something that it might have been worth trying to save.' Feeling her eyes smarting with oversensitive tears, Milly started to twist away.

Gianni reached out for her and pulled her into his arms, refusing to be held at bay by her resistance. 'Don't tear us apart with this,' he said unevenly. 'I made some mistakes. OK, I made a bloody *huge* mistake, but the minute I found out that you'd left Paris, I began looking for you.'

Milly was mutinous, unreachable. 'Because you had your child as an excuse. If it hadn't been for Connor, I'd still be out there, *lost*!'

'You're getting very worked up about this. You don't know what you're saying,' Gianni told her with stubborn conviction. 'OK, I didn't behave the way I should have after that business with Stefano, but once I came to terms with that—'

'Can't you even admit that you were *hurt*, like anybody else would?' Milly demanded emotionally, watching his devastatingly handsome features freeze and aching at the knowledge that he still wouldn't lower his barriers and let her in. 'Or did you stick me in a little compartment and just close the lid? Did you even manage to deal with it at all?'

Gianni's lean hands slid from her with a pronounced jerk. 'I'm going out for a while.'

'No, you are *not*! You walk out of this house now and you'll find barricades up when you try to walk back!' Milly warned him furiously.

'You are really angry with me right now. I have got nothing to say in my own defence,' Gianni spelt out thickly, rigid as a block of wood facing a very hungry bonfire. 'You haven't even given me the chance to apologise for misjudging you!'

'I don't want an apology. I accept that it looked bad for me that night. I accept that you were already jealous and so that much more likely to misinterpret what you saw. I even accept that Stefano is a convincing liar, and that you trusted him more than you could trust me.'

Gianni elevated an ebony brow with the kind of attitude that made her want to strangle him, stunning dark eyes coolly enquiring. 'So what *can't* you accept?'

'An emotional vacuum when we could have so much more!' she responded tautly.

'Enough is never enough for you, is it?'

'I'm not playing our marriage by your rules any more. Once I took all the risks, once I was the one who always went out on a limb...now it's your turn. I think I might enjoy seeing how good you are at expressing anything without sex.'

'Probably pretty hopeless,' Gianni admitted, disconcerting her. 'You want to humiliate me to pay me back for not believing in you three years ago.'

'Gianni...do you really think I'd do that to you?'

Gianni swung on his heel and strode out of the room. Milly emitted a strangled sob, suddenly wondering where all those crazy demands had come from and whether there was a certain unlovely grain of truth in his contention that she was trying to extract revenge.

She rubbed her eyes, knew she was smearing mascara everywhere, and finally she went off in search of Connor to console herself. But Gianni had got there first. He was in the playroom, sitting on the carpet in front of their son.

'Does she ask you how you're feeling all the time?' Gianni was asking broodingly while he set out Connor's toy train set. 'Does she want to know your every thought too?'

Connor gave him a winsome smile. 'Biscuit?' he said hopefully.

'Yes, I suspect that when you share your thoughts with Mamma it works very much to your advantage. Instant wish-fulfilment,' Gianni breathed reflectively. 'Do you think it could work that way for me?'

Milly reeled back against the wall outside the room and struggled to contain her laughter. But they looked so sweet together. Gianni chatting away, Connor giving up on the biscuit idea and getting down to play trains with all the accompanying choo-choo noises.

An hour later, Gianni walked into their bedroom. Fresh out of the shower, wrapped only in a towel, Milly fell still. Gianni sent her a disturbingly wolfish grin, exuding confidence in megawaves. 'Right, what do you want me to start talking about?'

'Us?' she practically whispered.

Gianni breathed in deep.

The silence was thunderous.

Milly couldn't bear it any longer. 'Why did you keep the house in Paris?'

'If you had ever decided to come back, you had to have somewhere to come back to,' Gianni pointed out levelly.

'But in all this time you hadn't changed anything at all!'

Gianni shrugged. 'Yes, I kept it like a shrine.'

Milly was poleaxed.

'When I wanted to feel close to you, I went there and sat for a while. I never stayed over. I used a hotel. Next question,' Gianni encouraged, as if he was competing in a fast and furious game.

'If you weren't able to talk to me like this before, how are you managing it now?' Milly whispered, wide-eyed.

'I've got to trust you. You're my wife.' Gianni breathed rather jerkily, as if that question had gone a little too deep.

Milly sighed. 'I've been so stupid. You wouldn't share things before because you thought I'd succumbed to Stefano.'

'I was protecting myself. I've probably protected myself more with you than any other woman,' Gianni admitted tautly, his strong facial bones now taut beneath his bronzed skin. 'Right from the start, I was vulnerable with you. Every time I walked away, I seemed to double back. I didn't like that. I didn't like the fact that I wasn't in full control.'

'But you were when you kept quiet?'

'It wasn't deliberate.' Gianni grimaced, his wide, sensual mouth tightening. 'You're always analysing emotions. I had learned to tune mine out and I was basically quite content like that. And when I met you you made it easy for me to go on that way. You knew what I wanted or what I didn't want before I had to say it. I didn't have to make an effort until you told me you were pregnant, and then you suddenly went silent and we were in trouble. One voice became no voice, *cara mia*.'

Milly was shaken by a truth she had never faced before.

'I'd always tried to *show* you that I cared, but all of a sudden that didn't seem to be enough. I really felt the change in you. I kept stalling on asking you to marry me,' he confessed ruefully. 'I didn't want you to say yes just because of the baby. I could see you weren't happy. That's why I became so jealous of Stefano. The cracks had appeared before he came along.'

'Yes,' Milly acknowledged, shaken yet again by his ability to put matters in their proper context. She *had* been different those last few months. 'I felt very insecure.'

'So you stopped telling me you loved me.' Gianni released a rather hollow laugh. 'You got me hooked on you saying it all the time and then you stopped. Considering that I never returned the favour, you had remarkable staying power, but I did wonder what was going on with you. I thought possibly you blamed me for getting you pregnant—'

'Oh, no!' Milly was pained by that misconception.

'So I tried not to mention the baby too much. I felt guilty. Of course I did,' Gianni shared heavily. 'I think I took those risks with you because on a subconscious level I was trying to push myself into making a real commitment to you.'

'But you were so upset when I told you I was pregnant.'

'I was scared I wouldn't live up to the challenge of being a parent,' Gianni admitted grimly.

'Gianni, you're a wonderful father,' Milly told him hotly.

'I'm learning.' Gianni shrugged, as if she had embarrassed him, brilliant beautiful dark eyes glimmering. 'You were right downstairs. I did let you down three years ago. I'm not proud of my behaviour. I'm ashamed that I listened to my brother instead of you. But I knew I could cope with him and I wasn't at all sure I could cope with you. And that word "hurt" doesn't cover what I was going through at the time.'

'I know.' Milly closed the distance between them to slide her arms round his lean hard body and feel her own heart beating as fast as a war drum.

'No, for once I don't think you *do* know,' Gianni countered almost roughly, framing her cheekbones with possessive hands. 'When I saw you with Stefano it was like somebody had taken my entire life and just blown it away. You had become so much a part of me that being without you was like being torn violently in two. And the half of me that was left was barely functioning afterwards.'

Milly stared up at him with mesmerised blue eyes.

'It took me a long time to fall in love, and it took even longer for me to realise that I did love you.' Gianni studied her with a raw intensity of unashamed emotion that touched her to the heart. 'And by the time I got the message, you'd vanished.'

'You loved me…' A strangled sob escaped Milly. She was overwhelmed by the poignancy of that confession, three years too late. 'Oh, that's awful!'

Gianni stooped to lift her up into his arms and carry her over to the bed. 'I'm only expecting to talk,' he told her loftily. 'I only want to comfort you.'

He held her close and her towel slipped. He watched the full swell of her pale breasts rise and fall with the rapidity of her breathing and an earthy groan was suddenly wrenched from him.

'I haven't really got that much more to talk about,' Gianni added in roughened continuation. 'You already know just how determined I was to get you back once I found you again.'

'You wanted Connor.'

'Behind every terrified male lurks a big liar,' Gianni shared, splaying long fingers satisfyingly wide over her slim hips and easing her into the hard cradle of his long, powerful thighs. I told you it was Connor I was really after. I told myself it was only sex I was after. I kept on telling myself that I couldn't trust you and then kept on forgetting it. But what I really wanted was everything back the way it was.'

'Your proposal really offended and hurt me…' Milly planted a fleeting kiss to his stubborn jawline.

'So I was trying to be cool. I didn't want to serve myself up on a plate. I certainly didn't want you to know that I was desperate for you to agree because I still loved you. I was trying not to admit that even to myself at that stage.'

'Oh, Gianni…' Milly sighed ecstatically. 'That's *all* I ever wanted, you know.'

'You put me through more hoops than a circus trainer,' Gianni growled feelingly. 'You really were that basic. When I did what you wanted, I was rewarded. When I didn't, I got time out as punishment. The first six months I was with you was like living in an earthquake zone.'

Milly ran a hand with provocative intent along the extended length of one lean, muscular thigh and watched his wonderful eyes narrow to a sexy shimmer of wildly appreciative gold. 'But I always loved you,' she said winsomely in her own favour.

'I adore you,' Gianni groaned with a slight shudder. 'You're gorgeous and smart and sexy and demanding—'

'*Very,*' she asserted.

'I'll never let anything or anybody hurt you again.' The most soul-destroyingly beautiful smile curved Gianni's mouth as he looked down at her.

Her heart tilted on its axis, but she knew she still had something important to say. 'But you still have to look after your brother,' she told him gently.

'Are you out of your mind?' Gianni demanded, staggered by that assertion.

'He was acting like a guy on the edge of a breakdown today, and deep down inside you know he needs you to sort him out. I know the way he was behaving makes you cringe,' Milly continued, with lashings of soothing understanding in her steady gaze, 'but you're all he's got, so he's your responsibility.'

'You couldn't possibly forgive him for what he did!'

'Three years ago, for the space of a minute, he give me a really bad scare…but afterwards he was much more scared than I was. Really scared people are not naturally noble or strong or honest. Think it over.'

'How come you're so compassionate about him but so tough on me?'

'You're like a great big thriving jungle plant and he's

more of a stunted seedling that needs help and encouragement to grow.'

Gianni flung his well-shaped head back on the pillows, dark eyes glinting with appreciation and amusement. 'You really know how to massage a guy's ego, *cara mia*.'

'Yours…oh, yes.'

'Did you realise that I was incredibly hungry the night you dumped that apple thing in Paris?'

'No, but I'm glad to hear it.'

'You can make it again for me.'

'Maybe…' Milly parted her lips with a shiver of delicious expectancy as his sensual mouth drifted downward.

Gianni stilled. 'I don't think we're likely to have a problem in the communication department again,' he proclaimed with satisfaction.

Tempted to tell him that she'd listened to him rehearsing with their son, Milly reared up, pushed his powerful shoulders back to the pillows and moaned in near desperation. 'Please shut up and kiss me!'

Six days later, on Christmas Eve, Milly watched Gianni finish reading a story about Santa Claus and his reindeer to Connor. He was able to answer all Connor's questions. Not a bad performance for a male who had never known a real Christmas as a child, Milly reflected with shimmering eyes.

After tucking their drowsy son in, Gianni straightened with a wry grin. 'We'll never get him to bed this early next year. He'll understand much more than he does now.'

They went downstairs together. Milly thought over the past week. It had been very eventful. All the publicity generated by their marriage and her mistaken identification as Faith Jennings had had stunning results as far as the Jennings family were concerned. Their long-lost daughter had written her parents a tentative letter from her home in the north of Scotland.

Divorced, and with three young children, the real Faith had admitted that the longer time went on the more difficult she had found it to get back in touch. They had since talked on the phone and were planning to meet in the New Year. Robin and Davina were anxious about how that reunion might go, but determined to be accepting of their adult daughter's independence. Milly believed it would be a happy reunion, because Faith had sounded rather lonely in her letter.

Gianni had also gone to see Stefano. They had talked. Gianni had emerged from that discussion feeling rather guilty, never having quite appreciated just how much Stefano relied on his approval, or indeed how devastated Stefano had been when Gianni had stopped treating him like a brother and given him only financial support. It was early days yet, but Milly reckoned that the healing process had started.

Gianni surveyed the drawing room of Heywood House. All the formality and the cool elegance had been banished. In all the rooms Milly used seasonal throws, glittery embellishments, festive padded cushions, unsophisticated homemade log, autumn leaf and berry arrangements and streams of paper chains ruled. Gianni even had to suffer a large fluffy Santa Claus toy on his library desk.

And he just loved it all, he acknowledged with a rueful smile of appreciation. He just loved the rich colour and warmth she brought into her surroundings, her innate ability to transform a house into a real home. He set a small parcel wrapped in beautiful paper down in front of her. 'You get your real presents tomorrow, but this is just a trifle I picked up ages ago,' he admitted, half under his breath.

Milly ripped off the paper and found herself looking at a delicate golden angel inside a crystal snowstorm on an ornate base. 'Oh, Gianni…' she sighed extravagantly. 'This is exquisite! Where did you get it?'

'New York.'

'But you haven't been there since—'

'Last year,' Gianni admitted, bracing himself.

'But you hadn't even found me then!' Milly gasped, instantly leaping up to envelop him in frantic hugs and kisses.

As desire flashed between them to instantaneous heat, Milly jerked back a step. 'Sometimes I love you so much it just hurts, *but* we still have a sooty bootprint to make on the hearth, so that Connor can see which chimney Santa Claus used as an entrance,' she explained apologetically.

'Maybe with the number of chimneys we've got we should put a flag on the roof so that the old guy doesn't get confused,' Gianni suggested deadpan as he curved her smoothly back into the possessive circle of his arms, knowing that bootprints could be faked after midnight as well as before it.

'Magic, doesn't need flags, Gianni!'

Against the backdrop of the flickering firelight and the glittering tree, Gianni scanned her wide, loving smile with softened dark eyes and pulled her close. 'You're the magic in my life, *cara mia*. I love you.'

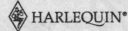

You're not going to believe this offer!

In October and November 2000, buy any two Harlequin or Silhouette books and save $10.00 off future purchases, or buy any three and save $20.00 off future purchases!

Just fill out this form and attach 2 proofs of purchase (cash register receipts) from October and November 2000 books and Harlequin will send you a coupon booklet worth a total savings of $10.00 off future purchases of Harlequin and Silhouette books in 2001. Send us 3 proofs of purchase and we will send you a coupon booklet worth a total savings of $20.00 off future purchases.

Saving money has never been this easy.

I accept your offer! Please send me a coupon booklet:

Name: _____

Address: _____ City: _____

State/Prov.: _____ Zip/Postal Code: _____

Optional Survey!

In a typical month, how many Harlequin or Silhouette books would you buy <u>new</u> at retail stores?

☐ Less than 1 ☐ 1 ☐ 2 ☐ 3 to 4 ☐ 5+

Which of the following statements best describes how you <u>buy</u> Harlequin or Silhouette books? Choose one answer only that <u>best</u> describes you.

☐ I am a regular buyer and reader
☐ I am a regular reader but buy only occasionally
☐ I only buy and read for specific times of the year, e.g. vacations
☐ I subscribe through Reader Service but also buy at retail stores
☐ I mainly borrow and buy only occasionally
☐ I am an occasional buyer and reader

Which of the following statements best describes how you <u>choose</u> the Harlequin and Silhouette series books you buy <u>new</u> at retail stores? By "series," we mean books within a particular line, such as *Harlequin PRESENTS* or *Silhouette SPECIAL EDITION*. Choose one answer only that <u>best</u> describes you.

☐ I only buy books from my favorite series
☐ I generally buy books from my favorite series but also buy books from other series on occasion
☐ I buy some books from my favorite series but also buy from many other series regularly
☐ I buy all types of books depending on my mood and what I find interesting and have no favorite series

Please send this form, along with your cash register receipts as proofs of purchase, to:
In the U.S.: Harlequin Books, P.O. Box 9057, Buffalo, NY 14269
In Canada: Harlequin Books, P.O. Box 622, Fort Erie, Ontario L2A 5X3
(Allow 4-6 weeks for delivery) Offer expires December 31, 2000.

PHQ4002